Protecting The Princess

(The Royals of Aldonia)

Nadine Millard

"YOU SHOULDN'T BE here, Your Highness."

Harriet Liezel Farago Wesselbach, Crown Princess of Aldonia spun around at the sound of the voice behind her, clutching a hand to her speeding heart.

"I – I was – that is—"

She stumbled to a halt under the scrutiny of the family's private butler, Ansel.

At only ten years old, Harriet was already well aware of what behaviours were acceptable for the Princess Royal.

It was just that occasionally she forgot.

Or chose to forget. She wasn't usually caught though.

"Your Highness, your father does not want anyone privy to his talks with the duke. Especially his children."

Harriet scowled up at the long-serving butler, who

was honestly more like a family member than a servant. At least to Harriet.

"But if Christopher wanted to listen—"

"His Royal Highness is heir to the throne, Highness. And more importantly, he is eighteen."

Harriet scowled but well, facts were facts, and everything Ansel said was true.

Heaving a sigh, she allowed him to guide her back to the private living quarters in the palace, away from where Father was conducting what sounded like a very tense meeting, if the shouting was anything to go by.

They hurried along the corridor surrounded by windows on both sides that led to the family's private quarters.

Harriet loved it here. In the summer, the sun warmed her skin in the glass hallway. In the winter, she could see snow for miles around. In the rainy season, the rain lashed against the windows and she sat for hours listening to the sound, watching the stormy clouds stream by.

She stopped now to watch the new recruits in her father's army march in formation around the courtyard.

Christopher was down there. She saw him, resplendent in his army blues, covered in medals and badges befitting the prince of the realm.

As she looked on, another figure arrived in the courtyard, bedecked in the blue jacket *sans* the medals and badges.

He skidded to a halt at the back of the last line of soldiers.

As Harriet watched, the formation ceased their marching and a tall, straight-backed figure stomped toward the straggler.

Even from up here she could tell the young man was in trouble. Harriet knew the feeling. She constantly seemed to find herself in trouble, too.

"Come along, Your Highness," Ansel coaxed Harriet away from the window.

The captain, or whomever the large man was, had turned and strutted back to the front of the soldiers. It appeared the young man was safe for now.

Just as Harriet was moving away from the window, the young soldier looked up. She was surprised by how fair he was. Golden hair glinted in the spring sunlight under his hat, and his skin was fairer than a lot of Aldonians', too.

He grinned up at her, delivering a flourishing bow, and Harriet giggled in response to his foolishness.

Before she could see if he would be taken to task for his antics, however, Ansel called out to her with practised patience.

Harriet dashed off ahead of the butler, wondering as she ran just who the golden-haired soldier could be. And why someone with such an apparent free spirit wanted to be a soldier, of all things.

Chapter One

*H*ARRIET LIEZEL FARAGO Wesselbach, Crown Princess of Aldonia, was bored.

There really was no other word for it.

Since her return from a winter in England where her older brother Alex had not only learned that he was to inherit a British earldom, but had also fallen in love *and* gotten married, she'd felt deflated.

While Alex had fallen in love, the most exciting thing Harriet had done was go to a ball.

The difference was stark and not at all pleasant to think on.

Whilst her oldest brother Christopher was in line to be king, and Alex was living a life of bucolic bliss rusticating in the English countryside, Harriet was wasting away in the gilded cage of Aldonia's royal palace.

She had the best of everything. She wanted for nothing.

Well, nothing except real friendships, a normal life—love.

Heaving a sigh of irritation at her own maudlin thoughts, Harriet threw her gothic novel onto the window seat she was occupying and jumped to her feet.

She turned to look out the open window, enjoying the feel of the cool spring breeze on her skin.

Watching the goings on in the gardens below was always somewhat interesting; members of court and politicians conversing in small clusters, the occasional servant scurrying from one task to another.

And there were her parents, King Josef and Queen Anya, taking a walk amongst their favourite Aldonian tulips.

Harriet's brow creased as she noticed her father's gait was slower, more lumbering than it used to be, and her stomach flip-flopped with worry.

Father had always been stern and distant. Being king would do that to a man, she supposed. But he was still her father, and she didn't like to think of him aging or becoming in any way frail or vulnerable.

Christopher was currently in France meeting—oh, someone terribly important, Harriet was sure. Truth be told, she probably didn't pay as much attention as she should to the goings on of Aldonia. Although even she had noticed the tension increase over the past few weeks. Her uncle, who had fallen foul of Papa years ago, had recently died and her cousin, his son Augustus, had been causing issues of some sort.

She didn't know what he was doing exactly or why.

But then, nobody would expect her to.

Her job was to be pretty and proper and charming to visiting dignitaries. That was it. That was the extent of her responsibility in life.

As she gazed out across the verdant palace lawns, a movement at the corner of the walled garden in which her parents were strolling caught her eye.

A solider in full regalia was moving briskly toward them.

Harriet frowned at the unusual sight.

Her parents rarely, if ever, wanted guards when in their gardens, preferring to have their time there as private as possible.

But this guard, whoever he was, was hurrying toward them with seeming determination.

A feeling of foreboding swept over Harriet, though she couldn't have said why.

There was just something—off about what she was watching.

Harriet glanced around the gardens but none of the other soldiers were even nearby, instead they were all at their stations. Where they should be.

She pressed her forehead to the window, keeping her deep-brown gaze trained on the renegade soldier.

And because she was looking so closely, she spotted the early spring sun glint off something in his hand. A dagger!

"No."

The word left Harriet on a horrified breath. Screaming would be useless. She was too far away, on the second floor of the palace. Yet what else could she do?

"Guards," she shouted at the top of her lungs, knowing someone would come running any second. But they would be in the same position as she; stuck here looking helplessly on.

The rogue soldier was nearing the perimeter of the gardens. She needed to do something!

Even now she heard the sound of footsteps coming. When a member of the royal family screamed, people came running.

But it wouldn't be enough to save her parents.

Harriet darted her eyes around, panic clawing at her, setting her heart thumping frantically and fear skittering along her veins.

Her gaze landed on an ornate vase. An heirloom that had been in her family for generations. Without a thought for the priceless artefact, she picked it up and threw it as hard as she could against the windowpane, which exploded with a loud crash.

Harriet leaned out as far as possible without tumbling out, supporting herself on the window frame, shards of glass digging into her flesh.

She looked straight to the small maze in which her

parents strolled, oblivious to the threat just feet away.

Harriet opened her mouth and screamed as loudly as she could, watching with relief as she caught the attention of people below.

"The king," she cried, even as soldiers and household staff skidded to a halt below her. "Get to the king."

Without stopping to question why, soldiers and parliamentarians alike turned and ran toward the flower mazes.

The would-be assassin had entered the maze by now, and Harriet nearly cast up her accounts as she watched him creep terrifyingly closer to her parents, the dagger now unmistakeable.

But Harriet's frantic warning was gaining traction and more and more people were running toward the maze.

Mercifully, her parents took notice. So, too, did the mysterious attacker.

Just as help arrived, the soldier turned and fled with a speed that seemed impossible, darting through the maze and out the other side.

Harriet's knees gave out as relief swept over her.

Her parents were safe.

But even as her maid Olga helped her regain her feet, even as household staff fussed around her whilst outside the king and queen were bustled into a crowd of protective guards, a knowing fear slithered along

Harriet's veins.

Someone wanted her father or mother dead. More than that, someone wanted the king or queen dead.

But why? And what on earth was going to be done about it?

Chapter Two

"THAT'S OUT OF the question, Christopher. And if Alex *does* come back to "collect me" as though I were a child, I'll tell him the same thing."

Harriet tried her best to keep her tone even, lest her overbearing older brother accuse her of hysteria. Again.

In the two weeks since the failed attempt on her parents' lives, the palace had been in turmoil. Harriet couldn't move without a guard trailing her, most social engagements had been cancelled, and now Christopher, who had returned from his trip to Paris, was acting like a dictator, demanding that Harriet be sent away like a recalcitrant child.

"Harriet, we've been through this." Christopher reached up to pinch the bridge of his nose, his black eyes serious and devoid of emotion.

Harriet felt a brief pang of guilt that she was adding to Christopher's rather enormous pile of stress.

As their father had been aging, Christopher had been taking on more and more duties in preparation for ascending the throne. And Harriet knew that the job of heir to the throne of Aldonia was a big enough mound of stress on her brother's relatively young shoulders.

Now they had an assassination attempt to deal with. And this just after Alex had rocked the kingdom to its core by moving to England to become an earl.

Not to mention the nasty split in the Wesselbach family, which was heating up again since her estranged uncle's death. Her cousin, the new Duke of Tallenburg, seemed determined to reopen old familial wounds, and Christopher as it turned out, had been trying to smooth things over with their odious cousin when the attack had taken place. That's why he'd been in Paris. Meeting their cousin on neutral ground, so to speak.

But much as Harriet could sympathise about the enormous strain Christopher was under, she wasn't about to have her life decided for her.

"Go to England with Alex and Lydia," Christopher said with practised patience. "And stay there a while. Just until we get to the bottom of whatever is going on here."

"I'm not a child, Christopher. You can't just send me off when—"

"For God's sake, Harriet. Do you not think I have enough to deal with without worrying about your safety, too?"

Harriet glared at her older brother, resenting the regal tilt of Christopher's chin, the cold anger in his dark eyes.

"I understand that you have a lot going on right now, Christopher. But sending me on a ship to England hardly seems a reasonable solution."

Christopher sighed wearily, and Harriet's resentment grew. She hated feeling as though she were an intractable infant.

But she hated even more feeling like an inconvenience that needed to be removed so Christopher could concentrate on the truly important issues.

This was her home. And she was his sister, for goodness sake. Not just a royal.

Ever since the attempted attack and Christopher's return home, there'd been a team of spies, agents, and soldiers working round the clock to figure out who had wanted her father dead, and if it was just the king or the entire family in danger.

Christopher had always erred on the side of caution in all of his actions, so it was no real surprise that he'd want her gone.

The problem was that he hadn't *asked* her if she'd leave before writing to Alex about it.

As soon as she'd found out, she'd written to Lydia, Alex's wife and Harriet's friend.

Do NOT let that great big oaf of a man come to collect me as though I were a child, she had written in anger, *and do NOT let Christopher bully either of you into thinking that Alex should leave you and the baby.*

Harriet had been thrilled when Lydia had written the news that she was expecting.

Originally, she had planned to travel back to Chillington Abbey to visit with Alex and Lydia, and spend time with her new niece or nephew.

Now however, wild horses wouldn't be able to drag her from Aldonia.

Her mother had always despaired of Harriet's stubborn streak.

Well, it was out in full force now.

"Let me be very clear." Christopher's tone was as rigid as the set of his shoulders. "I will be writing to Alex to tell him to ignore your childish letter to Lydia and to request that he do his duty to this family and come to escort you to England. If he has more sense than you, which wouldn't be difficult at this particular moment in time, he'll oblige."

Harriet gasped aloud at Christopher's juvenile insult, but her odious brother ignored her.

"Lady Althea has kindly agreed to have you stay at her family's home. It's closer to the docks and is therefore better suited to your travel plans. Now, I suggest you tell your maids what to pack for you. Because if you don't, I will."

Harriet was so enraged by Christopher's high-handedness that it took her a moment to process what he said, and when she did, she jumped to her feet, her daffodil skirts fluttering around her feet.

For a moment she could only glare at her brother, the only sound breaking the tense silence in his office the ticking of the ornate longcase clock in the corner.

But then, she found her voice.

"I can tell you with absolute certainty, Christopher, that I will *not* be going anywhere with Althea Furberg. And I will definitely *not* be staying with that family."

Christopher's eyes narrowed at Harriet's obvious display of dislike for Althea and her snivelling family.

They were the most sinfully sycophantic people Harriet had ever met.

From her infancy, the family had grovelled at the feet of the royal family at every opportunity. And Harriet wouldn't mind, if any of it seemed sincere.

But the Furbergs were the epitome of social climbers.

And for the last couple of years, Althea had clearly had her sights firmly set on Christopher. Nothing could mean more to the raven-haired woman, Harriet was sure, than a chance to become Queen of Aldonia.

And the worst of it was that Christopher seemed completely blind to the woman's machinations.

If Althea were a fiery, tempestuous beauty like Lydia Charring, Harriet might be able to understand.

Alex had fallen in love with Lydia from the moment she'd burst into that drawing room at Chillington Abbey covered in leaves and twigs. Harriet had seen it, though Alex had denied it for a time. And her romantic heart had swelled as she'd watched her beloved brother and Lydia fall in love.

But this? Christopher and Althea?

Harriet despaired of the potential match.

When they'd been younger, Christopher had been just as fun-loving as Alex, though he had always been the most serious of the siblings. Understandable, given he'd been raised from birth to run the country. But the point was he had a personality!

Althea Furberg had the personality of the chair Harriet had been occupying moments ago. How the lady hadn't bored her brother into a grave by now, Harriet didn't know.

Christopher clearly liked the fact that Althea never said or did, or probably even *thought* the wrong thing. But Harriet didn't like it for him. She loved Christopher. She wanted him to find a woman with spark, and wit, and—and the ability to form a thought that wasn't vacuous and ingratiating.

It suited Christopher's role as heir to the throne, this lack of any sort of interesting character, any sense of adventure in Althea Furberg. But it did *not* suit

Harriet or what she believed Christopher needed in a wife. And she'd be damned if she'd waste weeks of her life with the Furberg family awaiting Alex's arrival to drag her off to England.

"This conversation is over, Harriet."

It was as though she hadn't voiced any objection at all, Harriet thought bitterly.

"The Furbergs will arrive by the end of the week to escort you to their home. With a full guard, of course. And there you will await Alex's arrival."

"But—"

"Enough," Christopher snapped, and his tone was so commanding that Harriet fell immediately silent.

She watched as he heaved his big shoulders and stepped closer to her.

"Come now, Hari," he said, his voice calmer, regret glinting in his eyes. "You know I am only worried for your safety."

"I know," she sighed. Because as overbearing and even pompous as Christopher might be, he did truly care for her. Harriet knew that.

But she was mightily sick of people deciding things for her.

Her title decided the life she would live, even before she'd been born.

Her parents would decide whom she should marry. Being the only princess, Harriet's marriage would be used as a political alliance, just as soon as Father decided he wanted one.

And her overprotective big brothers decided nearly everything else for her.

Just once, Harriet would like to do something that *she* decided upon.

A sudden memory flashed in her mind's eye.

A line of regimental soldiers, not one of them with so much as a hair out of place.

And then, the rogue with the impish smile.

Harriet would just bet that a man like him wouldn't allow anyone to decide anything for him.

She had no idea if he was still a soldier, though she doubted it. A mischievous personality didn't exactly lend itself to army life.

Why he had popped into her mind at that moment, Harriet couldn't have said. But the memory of him triggered a sort of rebelliousness inside her.

For her whole life, Harriet had done exactly as she should. They all had. It came with the territory of being a royal.

The only time any of them had stepped out of line was when Alex had hidden the fact that he was a prince at all when he'd gone to England.

And look how that had turned out!

He was more in love with Lydia than anyone Harriet had ever seen, and he had a baby on the way. He was blissfully happy. And all because he'd followed his own path and not the one laid out for him.

"So, you'll go and pack?" Christopher asked, that steely determination in his voice.

"I will," Harriet agreed immediately. And she wasn't lying. She *was* going to go and pack. But she wasn't going anywhere with Althea's dreadful family.

She turned and hurried toward the door, her mind racing with possibilities.

"Hari."

Stopping at the sound of her brother's commanding voice, Harriet turned to see Christopher watching her with suspicion lighting his eyes.

"You won't do anything foolish."

It was a statement rather than a question, and once again, annoyance flickered to life within her.

"You've always been—impulsive," he continued. "But this isn't the time for that. I need you safe so I can concentrate on fixing this."

He needed her out of the way, he meant.

But Harriet didn't argue.

She gave her sweetest smile, trying to look as innocent as she could.

"I would never put myself in danger, Christopher," she assured him softly before darting from the room.

She had no idea if she'd convinced him or not.

But she didn't particularly have the time to worry about it.

Not if she was going to get out of here before the Furbergs arrived!

CHRISTOPHER STARED AT the space where his rebellious sister had stood before issuing a sigh that emanated from the depths of his soul.

It was difficult to be the Crown Prince and a big brother. Especially to one such as Harriet.

Her romantic notions and flair for adventure would get her in trouble if he didn't have her watched closely.

Allowing her to go to England with Alex had been a mistake, and he'd told their father as much.

Alex had always been the renegade and had proven that by taking up with Lydia Charring and deciding to rusticate in the English countryside, rather than seeing to any royal duties in Aldonia.

Christopher was happy for his younger brother, of course. He liked Lydia, and he'd never seen Alex so content.

And of course, that wasn't a twinge of envy he felt. He'd never minded being the heir to the throne, or the shackles of responsibility that came with it.

But in the last couple of years, those responsibilities had felt as though they were drowning him.

Firstly, with Father taking a step back, then with the renewed uneasiness in the truce with the Tallenburg family.

And now, a damned assassination attempt.

Christopher knew who he suspected. He'd be blind or completely stupid not to think his power-mad cousin was behind all of this. What he didn't know, however, was how his cousin would have gotten someone past the guards, or how he would have known about his father's routines and habits.

With everything going on, the last thing he needed to worry about was one of Harriet's flights of fancy.

She'd given her word, however, that she wouldn't do anything foolish.

So, it was a question of whether he trusted her or not, Christopher supposed.

Sighing again, Christopher moved to his desk, ringing for a footman with one hand, whilst removing a sheaf of his personal parchment from the other.

It was time to send for reinforcements.

But with someone in the palace leaking information, this particular letter wouldn't be going through any official channels.

Chapter Three

HARRIET ONCE AGAIN silently thanked her brother Alex for having insisted that they travel as commoners when they'd gone to England last year, for it lent her the experience needed for doing so now.

Christopher would be furious, she knew. Her parents worried. And honestly, she was worried herself. After all, there was a presumably skilled killer on the loose. One who had it in for the royal family.

And she was the only princess.

But Harriet had lived a relatively private life, confined to the palace or the homes of the peers of Aldonia.

She'd rarely travelled through the towns and villages of Aldonia, and certainly never without a royal guard and a full entourage of servants and maids.

The only time she'd travelled anywhere of consequence had been when she'd gone to England with

Alex. And being fussed over by one's big brother didn't feel remotely adventurous, she had learned.

So being alone now, she wouldn't draw much, if any attention. She hoped.

By the time she was missed, she planned to be as far from the palace as possible.

Harriet had no doubt that her actions would be viewed as careless, immature, and downright dangerous.

But she had meant what she'd said to Christopher the other day; she had no intention of putting herself in danger.

Equally though, she had no intention staying with the ghastly Furbergs.

And she certainly had no intention of forcing Alex to take her to Chillington Abbey so she could be underfoot and in the way whilst he tried to enjoy his new family.

Ever since Alex and Lydia had married, and Christopher had taken up more royal duties, Harriet had felt—dispensable.

With no real purpose and no real responsibility, she felt decidedly on the outskirts of her own life.

Knowing that Lydia and Alex would be forced to host her while they were trying to find their footing as new parents and a new family unit was humiliating.

Not only that, but it would serve to remind Harriet just how alone she really was in the world.

And it wasn't as though she could talk about such feelings. She could only imagine how breathtakingly spoiled she would sound should she confess to someone that her life of wealth and pampered privilege was unsatisfying. Lonely, even.

And so, here she was. Outside the palace, dressed in her least luxurious clothing and a cloak stolen from the servants' quarters.

She'd return it, of course, Harriet thought uncomfortably. Just as soon as she'd given Christopher enough time to solve the mystery.

She'd even buy a new, fur-trimmed one for whomever she'd stolen from.

And it wasn't as though she'd left whichever maid was a victim of her thievery empty-handed. She'd left a cloak of her own there.

The trundling sound of a coach interrupted Harriet's guilty thoughts, and she looked up to see the mail coach making its way slowly to the inn she stood awkwardly in front of.

She had worn her biggest bonnet so that her face would be hidden. She didn't think anyone would pay much attention to a young serving girl travelling alone but didn't want to take any chances either.

The coach drew to a halt, and the driver jumped down, shouting about a thirty-minute wait time.

Thirty minutes? Drat. Harriet thought.

She didn't have thirty minutes.

NADINE MILLARD

If Christopher found her note sooner than Harriet hoped, he'd send a hundred soldiers chasing after her.

Probably lock her in the tower, too, for good measure.

And yet, what choice did she have?

She couldn't very well walk to the Winter Palace. Travelling by coach, especially public coach, would take days.

Walking would be impossible.

Especially given the fact that she'd had to pack every sort of supply she'd been able to steal from the kitchens in the last couple of days, and she now had two stuffed valises and no way of carrying them.

Sneaking out this morning on one of the gigs Alex had left behind had been hard enough.

She only hoped that someone would come and rescue the horses she'd stolen sooner rather than later.

The temptation to take them all the way to the palace in Gant had been nearly overwhelming, but it was far too conspicuous. The guard would catch her before she'd even left the capital. No, she had to travel by public coach.

Harriet wasn't stupid enough to stay at the Winter Palace, of course.

But there was an old, disused woodcutters' cottage in the wilderness that bordered the grounds, and there she intended to stay until Christopher stopped trying to get rid of her, and until the danger to her family had passed.

Nobody, not even her ladies-in-waiting, knew of Harriet's plans to travel there, so it was unlikely that anyone else would be able to find her.

In her youth, Harriet had spent weeks using the cottage as her own, personal hideout. No one ever seemed to know about it, no one ever seemed to go there but her. And she'd kept it a secret, even from Alex.

She didn't know who had owned it or why it was disused. It had sat there, hidden and vacant for as long as she could remember.

A babbling stream provided fresh, clean water from the mountains, and though she'd never spent time there when the ground wasn't thick with snow, she was fairly confident that firewood would be available in abundance.

She would be just fine, Harriet told herself. Even though she'd never before been alone nor had to fend for herself, she would be fine.

Harriet huffed out an impatient sigh and cast her gaze around the busy courtyard of the inn.

She took in the building, the people bustling about, and—

Her eyes skidded to a halt as she realised, with no small amount of dread, that she seemed to have drawn the attention of the most unsavoury looking man she'd ever seen.

"Oh, no," she whispered, fear making her clutch her reticule tighter.

Harriet turned her head away, but she could sense that he was still watching her.

She'd known, of course, that it was going to be risky making this journey alone. But she wasn't even out of the city yet!

"What's a pretty little thing like you doing all alone?"

Harriet felt a jolt of fear shoot through her as she realised the man had made his way closer.

Even with her back turned, she could smell the alcohol mixed with unwashed clothing and sweat emanating from the man.

Should she ignore him? Turn to face him?

Harriet had no idea how to deal with such behaviour. Barring one or two lascivious glances from visiting dignitaries, she'd never been exposed to unpleasant male behaviour. In point of fact, she'd never been much exposed to males at all. Kept at a distance befitting the Crown Princess, the only time she'd felt anything close to normal was when she and Alex had visited England and hidden their royal status.

Even then they'd travelled in private, relative luxury, and with a small retinue of servants.

And much as she'd envied the young women of Aldonia who lived a non-royal, freer existence than she, this part of things she really could have done without.

Mustering her courage and considerable diplomatic skills, Harriet turned to face her unwanted companion, hoping that a cool but pleasant smile and a request to be left alone would suffice to send him on his way.

But her smile stiffened then died as she turned and saw that he was watching her in a way that could only be described as predatory.

"Don't you talk then?" he slurred.

"I – I do," she stumbled, tightening her grip on the reticule that held her only coin. Coin she desperately needed.

"Where you off to all alone?" the man repeated, his eyes taking in the two bags at her feet.

"That's not really any of your business," Harriet answered with a boldness she didn't feel.

The bloodshot eyes that were studying her filled with an ominous menace.

"I can make it my business," he threatened softly, putting the fear of God into her.

"Sir," Harriet could hear the accent she'd tried to adopt slipping, could hear that she was sounding more imperious by the second. "I suggest you take yourself elsewhere. I have no interest in speaking to you further."

She watched in horror and no small amount of trepidation as the blackguard raked an insolent gaze over her then promptly burst into a peal of laughter, spittle flying from a mouth absent of several teeth.

"Sounds like you could do with learning some manners, my lady," he sneered, the moniker clearly meant as a jeer.

"I—"

Whatever Harriet had been about to say was cut off with her outraged gasp as the man suddenly reached out and grabbed her arm.

Harriet didn't know what to do. Screaming for help would draw too much attention to her, and her efforts to drag herself from the drunkard's grasp weren't doing any good.

"Sir, if you do not release me, I'll—"

Suddenly he leaned forward, and Harriet almost wretched from the stench radiating from him.

"You'll do what?" he smirked.

"Ah, there you are, sweetling. Please, forgive my delay in joining you. Made a new friend, have you?"

Harriet spun around at the sudden sound of a jovial voice behind her.

There stood the handsomest man she'd ever seen. Though his clothing was simple, it was well made and clean, leading her to believe that he was a merchant of means or perhaps a modest gentleman.

She could only stare at him, taking in the golden blonde hair, the shockingly blue eyes.

Something about him was familiar, though she

knew they'd never met before. She would have remembered.

So distracted by his chiselled jaw was Harriet, that it took a moment for his words to sink in, and when they did, she was more confused than ever.

Was everyone in Aldonia mad?

Between the blackguard accosting her and the handsome stranger acting as though they were—well, that she was his *sweetling*, Harriet was fit to scream and run back to the safety of the palace.

She turned her gaze to the drunk's and saw that his own was now darting warily between Harriet and the stranger.

"Ahem."

The sound of the golden-haired man clearing his throat brought Harriet's eyes back to him, and she noted that though his expression remained neutral, his eyes, as they took in the drunk's hand still on Harriet's arm, were coldly dangerous.

Without speaking a word, those same eyes rose to meet the drunkard's, and Harriet almost felt sorry for the man, so lethal was the look.

"I assume you don't want this man's hand on you, my dear?" The stranger's tone was soft and would have been pleasant, if it wasn't for the dangerous edge to it.

Just who *was* this man?

Guessing that she was "his dear" though she had no idea who he was, Harriet managed to shake her head.

"Um, no," she answered.

She had no idea what the stranger was up to, but there was an air of authority about him that made Harriet feel secure in his presence. Strangely enough, she trusted him though that was probably rather foolish, given the fact that he was an unknown to her just like the drunkard.

But she instinctively knew that her chances of safety were far better with the blonde man helping her than the drunk one threatening her.

"And you." He turned to her would-be harasser. "I assume you would like all of your limbs to stay attached to your body?"

Harriet felt her jaw drop at the words, so softly spoken, so calm.

"Er—yes?"

The attacker sounded as confused as Harriet felt.

"Excellent." The man was all politeness and joviality once again. "Then remove your hand from her arm, and remove yourself from the vicinity, and we'll all get what we want."

Harriet's arm was immediately released as the drunk stumbled backwards.

"I – I didn't know that she – that you and she—"

"Well, now you do," the man quietly interrupted the slurred rambling. "So, be on your way."

Harriet watched in both relief and confusion as her harasser beat a hasty retreat, nearly falling over himself as he stumbled away.

The silence in his wake was deafening.

Harriet turned once more to stare in consternation at the overly familiar man.

The grin on his face could charm birds from the trees.

But Harriet was too bemused and frankly put out at his high-handedness to be charmed.

"Now that that's sorted, perhaps you would like to join me for some refreshments?" he asked.

Harriet could only gaze in amazement as he bent and plucked up her luggage, one bag in each hand, as though they weighed nothing at all.

"Shall we?" He smiled, acting for all the world as though they were the greatest of friends or—she swallowed nervously—or something else.

Without awaiting an answer, he turned and headed toward the inn.

Harriet closed her jaw with a snap as her irritation exploded to full anger.

"Excuse me," she called in her haughtiest tone. "Just who are you and where do you think you're going with my belongings?"

Chapter Four

*J*ACOB LAUER WORKED harder than he should have to control his irritation at Princess Harriet's affronted tone.

Ever since he'd received the missive from the Crown Prince himself the other day, the missive that had him swearing in every language in his repertoire, he'd been dreading this particular assignment.

In fact, he'd been seconds from writing back to Prince Christopher to inform the man in no uncertain terms, that he was a spy, a solider, even an assassin if the situation warranted it. But not, under any circumstances, a nanny.

Especially for a pampered, privileged princess.

But common sense, and a talk with his oldest friend and confidante, led him to change his mind.

"You can't say no to a direct request from the Crown Prince of Aldonia, Jacob," Hans said in that irritatingly reasonable tone. *"Besides, she's the Crown Princess. It*

will be a day or two at most before she runs back to the palace and her luxurious life. You'll be back to a real assignment within a week. Finding out who the hell wants the royal family dead."

Much as Jacob would have loved to argue, he'd known his friend was right.

So here he found himself, pretending to bump into the princess outside a coaching inn.

It turned out that her brother's concerns had been well founded. For Jacob had been watching her since he'd received Prince Christopher's letter two days past.

He'd watched her skulk around the kitchens after dark. He'd watched her thieving little hands steal a cloak from the servants' quarters.

And then he'd watched this morning as she'd snuck from the palace at the break of dawn. On the very day the Furbergs were due to come and take her to safety.

Jacob had looked on, half amused, half annoyed that the lady was going to be more hassle than he'd hoped for, as she'd dragged two bags out the servant's entrance of the kitchens.

She'd been spotted by the guards almost immediately, of course, and only Jacob's intervention had stopped them from marching her back inside. Prince Christopher knew his sister well and had instructed Jacob that if Harriet ran, he was to follow, not stop her.

The prince had offered a brief explanation, though

Jacob supposed he didn't have to.

"My sister is—tenacious," the prince had explained with an air of exasperation that Jacob knew only a female could inspire. *"If she has decided to run, then nothing will stop her. I'd rather you kept an eye on her than have her sent with the Furbergs and then go missing near the ships."*

Jacob understood the prince's plan, even as he resented being the one to have to implement it.

So instead of the royal guards doing their jobs, he'd stepped in and told them to allow the princess to leave.

That same intervention had led to the lady thinking she'd managed to escape unnoticed, of course. And had given her a misplaced sense of confidence in her abilities to blend in.

It wasn't just that she'd very obviously never been out alone, and certainly had never travelled alone. But she was so damned beautiful that she'd draw attention to herself dressed in rags. A fact that was sure to add to the difficulty of Jacob's job.

Jacob hadn't meant to make his presence known until he'd tailed her to wherever it was she was planning on going.

But he'd spotted the wastrel in the courtyard long before Princess Harriet had, and when the man had staggered toward her, Jacob hadn't had much choice but to get involved.

With his plan to stay unnoticed now an impossibility, he had to think on his feet.

Something that was proving difficult in the face of the princess's distractingly big brown eyes.

Ensuring that his face was a friendly but emotionless mask, Jacob turned back to face the fuming Princess Harriet.

Her outrage was exasperating. Didn't she realise what could have happened if he hadn't intervened?

His method had been a little unorthodox, but that was only because he wanted to avoid a scene.

And shooting the opportunistic blackguard between the eyes definitely would have caused a scene.

Prince Christopher wanted his sister dealt with subtly and without notice. Again, the body of a drunken lout would definitely have been noticed.

The princess was glaring at him, her eyes filled with both affront and bewilderment.

"Forgive me." Jacob sketched a bow, her bags swaying against his legs. "I felt it prudent to step in when I thought you might be in danger. It's not safe for a woman to travel alone, Miss."

"Apparently not, given I've had one man try to accost me and now another stealing my bags."

Jacob bit back a reluctant grin. She was feistier than he would have expected.

He suddenly remembered one morning a lifetime ago when he'd been trying his best to become a disciplined royal guard.

He'd been late to drills. Again. And was suffering the wrath of his captain. Again.

He'd looked up and seen Princess Harriet, then only a child of ten compared to his eighteen years, gazing down at the courtyard.

And he'd briefly wondered what life would be like for the little princess given that it would be even more regimented than that of a soldier. If she did have a free spirit, it would be sure to have disappeared before she was in long skirts, he'd thought with a pang of sadness for the girl.

Jacob knew all about the detriment of a free spirit.

As the second son of the Count of Dresbonne, it had been expected of him to climb the ranks to become an estimable lieutenant.

Unfortunately for the count, his son's personality did not lend itself to the strictures of army life.

Fortunately for Jacob, he proved himself skilled enough in areas that led to a far more exciting and lucrative, but far more dangerous life than that of a soldier.

He'd become one of an elite group of agents reporting directly to Prince Christopher himself.

He'd thought that his current assignment would be tracking down and disposing of the would-be assassin who'd come for the royal family not a week ago.

When he'd received Prince Christopher's missive

the other evening, he'd assumed that he was being sent to find out who inside the palace could have been leaking information about the king's private routine, and who would have sent a man to kill him.

But no.

The letter had been akin to a request for a governess for the princess.

Jacob had never spent any time with the princess. The nature of his work meant he spent more time out of Aldonia than he spent within her borders, and when he was around, he tended to avoid Society events that involved the royals and the peerage, lest he inadvertently embarrass his father, or accidentally get bored to death.

He'd heard of the princess's beauty, of course. And her grace. Her decorum. Her charitable endeavours.

In short, she'd sounded as boring as every other lady of Society. The only difference being the crown on her head.

But this outraged young woman, with her hands planted firmly on her hips, and her deep brown eyes glinting with fire, didn't look like any other dull lady. And she wasn't anywhere near a crown, or the security that came with one.

"I'm not stealing your bags, Miss." He offered his most charming smile, which only served to have her eyes narrow further.

Jacob felt his own patience begin to wear thin.

He was still trying to figure out what to do now that he'd blown his cover. He didn't need her recalcitrance right now.

"I just thought that perhaps you would be more comfortable sitting inside having some refreshments while you waited for the coach."

She eyed him speculatively.

"I didn't think it prudent for me to enter such an establishment alone." She sounded a little defensive, and very untrusting, which was understandable given the circumstances.

It also proved that she had at least a modicum of sense about her, although if that were true, she hardly would have snuck from the palace unnoticed in the first place. Or thought she did.

"But you are not alone. At least not any longer." He smiled.

Maybe he was losing his touch. But she looked completely unmoved by what he had thought was his most charming expression.

"Being with a complete stranger is hardly safer, or more prudent, than being alone," she sniffed.

Jacob gritted his teeth and strove for patience.

They'd spent so long standing here arguing that the bloody coach would set off again by the time he'd persuaded her to get inside to relative safety and anonymity.

Prince Christopher would be less than pleased if

the Crown Princess were to be discovered alone at a coaching inn.

"There is a very easy solution to that." He kept his tone light but not flirtatious. He couldn't afford to scare her off. "We can use the time until the coach leaves to get to know each other, and then we'll no longer be strangers."

"That would still require me to go with you, currently a stranger, in order to become acquainted enough with you for you *not* to be a stranger any longer."

My God. The woman would argue with a brick wall.

Jacob found himself in the unusual position of not knowing quite what to do.

Ever since he'd begun working for the Crown, he'd taken every assignment in his stride. He was a crack shot, an excellent swordsman, and he was possessed of a sharp mind.

He knew how to uncover state secrets, how to weed out traitors to the Crown, he could kill a man with his bare hands if necessary, and travel through Europe undetected.

But damned if he could find a way to get this diminutive, spoilt bunch of outrage inside that inn.

And now that they'd already "met," he didn't know how he'd keep her safe when she got to wherever she was going.

He could lurk in the shadows of course, but that could mean potentially not being close enough should someone attack her.

So his idea of being a townsperson wherever she landed, and befriending her gradually while also keeping an eye on her, had disappeared with the drunk he'd run off.

His head was beginning to ache, and he still had no real plan.

Perhaps it was time to take a bit of a gamble.

Jacob placed the bags back on the ground.

"Though our meeting is a little unorthodox, and certainly not as appropriate as I would like, allow me to introduce myself." He sketched a perfectly polite bow. "My name is Jacob Lauer, and I am taking the coach to Gant." He saw no harm in giving her his real name as he named the closest village to the Royal Winter Palace, which was where he figured she was going from the coach she was planning to take.

He had no doubt she wasn't silly enough to actually stay at the palace, but even when people were running they craved some level of familiarity, so she could perhaps be using it as a stop gap. Plus this particular coach travelled to that town. It was an educated guess and he could only hope he was right.

"I was raised in a family of sisters and I'm afraid that my protective instincts caused me to act in a way that was perhaps not entirely proper. But now that you are safe and happy to remain alone, I shall leave you to it. Have a pleasant trip, Miss."

He turned on his heel and walked toward the inn, all the while hoping that his gamble would pay off.

He'd taken more steps than he was happy about when she finally called out.

"Wait."

Just one word, more command than request, but she was used to ordering people about, he supposed.

Jacob ensured there was no trace of triumph on his face before he turned back around.

Chapter Five

$\mathcal{H}$ARRIET DIDN'T KNOW if she was making a mistake or not, but the truth was that the encounter with the drunk had scared the wits out of her and this man, though he seemed rather arrogant, also seemed rather capable.

He'd mentioned sisters, too, which somewhat put her mind at ease. Even if it shouldn't.

And truth be told, she trusted him.

She didn't know if it was those big shoulders of his that looked as though they could carry the weight of the world.

Maybe it was just that she felt completely and utterly lost and wanted so badly to lean on someone, just for a moment.

He could be worse than the drunk, for goodness sake! Yet she didn't think so.

Wondering at her own sanity, Harriet called out and braced herself for a look of smug triumph.

Yet when Mr. Lauer turned around, his expression was as friendly and polite as ever.

"P-perhaps I might enjoy some tea," she said grudgingly.

His smile was a thing of beauty, but Harriet could not allow herself to notice such things. She needed to keep her wits about her.

"Excellent, allow me then. Miss?" He bent and plucked up her bags again as though they weighed nothing.

Harriet was about to give him her name when she stopped.

Good heavens! She didn't know what to call herself!

All of her careful planning, and she hadn't come up with a pseudonym.

Though she hadn't actually been planning on speaking to anyone, in her defence. Lonely, perhaps. But preferable to being sent away or having to endure the company of Althea Furberg.

His raised brow indicated that he found her hesitation odd.

"Harriet," she blurted. "Harriet – er – Royal."

She almost cringed as the embarrassing name popped into her head. Apparently subterfuge wasn't one of her strong suits.

Still, it was done now and couldn't be taken back.

She thought that she detected a hint of amusement

in his blue eyes as she introduced herself, but when she looked again, his expression was nothing more than friendly and polite.

"Shall we, Miss Royal?"

Still wondering if she was making a huge mistake, Harriet nevertheless nodded and followed him to the entrance of the bustling inn.

When he hefted one of her bags to the other arm, holding them both in an easy grip whilst pushing open the door for her, Harriet couldn't help but admire his strength and his manners. Perhaps he wasn't as arrogant as he had first appeared.

As she stepped inside, she glanced around the room, fascinated but not entirely comfortable with the tableau before her.

The din of conversation was interrupted frequently with raucous male laughter. The savoury smell of cooking meat battled with the smell of ale and sweat, interspersed every now and then with the cloying perfume of serving girls who flitted from table to table carrying tankard-laden trays whilst swatting away roving hands.

The entire thing was a spectacle, and one she'd never witnessed before.

The feel of a hand on the small of her back startled her, and she turned to see Mr. Lauer smiling down at her.

"Wait here a moment." He leaned in to speak in

her ear, and Harriet almost grew dizzy inhaling the sandalwood and spice scent surrounding him. "I'll be right back."

The gooseflesh that broke out on her skin just from the man's proximity was ridiculous, and Harriet spent the few moments that he was away giving herself a stern talking to about it.

Dragging in a mouthful of not entirely pleasant air, she watched him speak swiftly to who she assumed was the proprietor and give him a handful of coin.

Within seconds he was back and picking up her bags once more, the portly landlord bustling after him.

"If you'll follow me, sir, miss." He grinned at them both before leading the way through the lively crowd to a small wooden door.

He swung open the door then stepped back to allow Harriet inside the room.

She couldn't help but breathe a sigh of relief when she walked through to the small, private dining room.

There was a fire crackling in the hearth in front of which stood a highly polished table and four chairs.

"I thought you'd be more comfortable in here." Mr. Lauer smiled at her before turning to the landlord. "My wife and I are awaiting the coach," he announced, and Harriet felt her jaw drop. His *wife*? "If you could bring a tea tray, some breads, cheeses, and cold meats, I'd be much obliged. And quickly, please. We don't have much time."

With a bow, the landlord moved to do Mr. Lauer's bidding, leaving them quite alone.

"Your wife?" Harriet asked tartly.

His answering grin seemed vaguely familiar, but Harriet couldn't concentrate enough to wonder why. She was too distracted. The man had dimples, for heaven's sake! As if he needed dimples to add to his handsomeness.

"I didn't think it appropriate to have him know you were dining alone with a man you'd only just met," he answered smoothly.

"Oh. Y-yes, of course," she stammered. She really should have thought of that herself. In truth, Harriet had never had to do much thinking for herself. Or been allowed to. Even when she and Alex had travelled to England and hidden the fact that they were royals, she'd been under Alex's protection for the duration.

"Come, make yourself comfortable, Miss Royal. It will be twenty minutes yet before the coach arrives. Plenty of time to eat and relax."

"Thank you," Harriet said primly, removing her stolen cloak and bonnet, desperately hoping that he wouldn't recognise her.

She stood awkwardly holding them before he reached out and plucked them from her grip, resting them on a bench against the wall before moving to hold out a chair for her.

She smiled her thanks before sitting and nervously

wringing her hands.

"You have nothing to worry about, Miss Royal," he announced, taking a seat across from her. "I only want to see you comfortable before you make the trip to—wherever it is you're going."

His smile seemed genuine, his countenance innocent. And his shockingly blue eyes gave no indication of recognition. Harriet could see no reason not to trust that what he said was true.

"Why should you care for the comfort of a stranger?" she asked.

"Because it is the gentlemanly thing to do," he said smoothly before his mouth curled up in a wicked grin. "The fact that the stranger is such a beautiful one is merely a bonus," he continued, right as the door opened and a maid bustled in with a tray.

JACOB COULD HAVE kicked himself as he watched a delicate blush stain Princess Harriet's cheeks. But he found himself in the unusual position of being distracted whilst on a mission, and it had slipped out before he'd quite known what he was about.

He took the time whilst the maid set the tray down and began to unload the teapot, cups, and plates of food, to get a hold of himself.

Yes, he *was* distracted by Princess Harriet. By those

eyes, that hair, the unusual mix of strength and vulnerability in her. Though he considered a princess running off alone the height of folly, he knew it took a certain amount of courage to do so.

She had wit, too. Her choice of name proved that.

But none of that was relevant to the job at hand.

His job was to keep her safe, not admire her beauty or spirit.

Princes Harriet set about pouring tea whilst Jacob filled a plate and pushed it toward her before filling his own.

"So." He kept his tone casual as the maid took her leave and left them alone. "Are you from Gant, or just visiting?"

Her eyes shot up to his, and once again a delicate blush blossomed on her cheeks.

"Oh, I – uh. I live there."

Jacob nearly smirked. She wasn't very good at this. She'd never actually told him where she was going. But his guess, as it turned out, had obviously been right. And an imp of devilment awoke in him.

"How wonderful. I shall be sure to call on you then, since I intend to stay awhile in the village."

"No!" she blurted. "I – that is you – well, I, I don't *live* there. I mean, I *did* live there. Once. Before. But now, I don't." She stumbled to an awkward silence before lifting her cup to her mouth.

Jacob averted his eyes lest he get distracted by her

lips blowing on the liquid, on top of everything else vying for his attention.

"So you are just visiting then?" he prompted.

Honestly, who ran away in disguise without even a decent cover story? Jacob began to see why Prince Christopher was insistent on a minder for the girl.

"Yes. No," she stuttered before heaving a big sigh. "I am visiting but not for long. So – so you wouldn't be able to call on me or, or even see me really, since it is a very short visit."

He almost felt sorry for her when he heard the desperation in her tone.

"Your family are not worried about you travelling alone then?" he asked softly, watching her reaction.

Her face blanched as her eyes widened.

"M-my family?"

"Yes, your family," he repeated. "After all, it is obvious that you are gently bred Miss Royal, and I cannot imagine that your family would happily leave you unprotected."

That mouth popped open and Jacob watched in amusement as her dark gaze darted around the small dining room, as though a suitable answer would be lurking in a corner somewhere.

"I don't have a family. They're dead." She winced as she said it, and he could only imagine that she was suffering some sort of guilt for saying such a thing.

"You are alone in the world then."

Her eyes shot back to his and narrowed slightly and she huffed out a breath, scowling with obvious irritation.

"I am not alone," she said. "I – I am on my way to a governess post. For a very prominent family. A family who is expecting me and will send someone to look for me should I not arrive on time. My time in Gant is just a brief stop to – um – rest before continuing the journey," she finished weakly.

Ah, so she'd suddenly decided to think of her safety then.

"And I wasn't asked this many questions in my interview for the post," she tacked on tartly.

"I'm glad to hear it." He smiled in what he hoped was a reassuring manner, ignoring her pointed comment. "This world isn't a safe one for a young woman alone."

"The world doesn't seem to be safe for anyone at the moment." She spoke softly, but Jacob heard every word and for the first time, he allowed himself to think of how scared Princess Harriet must be. For herself and her family.

Why on earth then would she run away and endanger herself?

Before he got a chance to ask any more questions however, a rap on the door signalled the arrival of the landlord with the message that the coach outside the inn was ready to depart.

Standing, Jacob held out a hand to the princess. "Shall we?"

She hesitated only a moment before she placed her gloved hand in his own.

Chapter Six

$\mathcal{H}$ARRIET HAD NEVER travelled by public coach before, and she hoped that she'd never have to again.

And she found herself more grateful than ever that she'd met Mr. Lauer. Even if he was a bit arrogant.

She didn't know what would have happened if she were completely alone. The other occupants squeezed into the conveyance would have scared her witless; she knew that much.

Just as she knew that she wouldn't have found the feel of their legs pressing against her own as exciting as she found Mr. Lauer's.

Harriet couldn't quite believe she was sitting here thinking of a stranger's legs instead of thinking of what she would do when the coach arrived in Gant. Truth be told, much as she was glad of the company and safety of having Mr. Lauer as a companion, provided he didn't turn out to be a murderer of course, she was worried about getting rid of him when their journey was at an end.

They wouldn't arrive in Gant until very early tomorrow morning.

With only one stop scheduled to change horses and give the passengers and driver a chance to eat and stretch their legs, sleep was something they would all have to forgo. Or so Harriet had thought.

Now, as she sat here pressed against the wall of the coach on one side and Mr. Lauer on the other, she watched the other passengers begin to drop off, their heads nodding about as though bobbing on water.

Harriet was pleased for the reprieve from either lascivious or openly hostile glances from the occupants, and she thanked her lucky stars once more that she'd been befriended by Mr. Lauer.

He'd once again managed to procure a private dining room for their dinner when they'd stopped and had even sent in a maid with a jug of fresh water to allow Harriet to freshen up. She would never have been able to enjoy relative comfort without him.

But now that they were mere hours from their final destination, she needed to figure out how to extricate herself from his company.

He was a gentleman, so she guessed that he would never leave without seeing to her safety. And lord only knew how she'd slip away with two heavy bags.

"You should try to sleep, Miss Royal."

His voice, lowered in deference to the time of night and their sleeping travel companions, had the oddest effect on Harriet. It sounded intimate, and her skin broke out in gooseflesh. All her reactions to him were most inappropriate. And inconvenient.

"Oh, I – I'm not tired," she lied.

She was exhausted, truth be told. And when they got to Gant, she had to face a walk that would take half a day at least. Alone. And trying to manage her hefty luggage.

It had been easier to be excited about her adventure when she'd been in the comfort of the palace, she thought wryly.

"Tell me, will there be someone to meet you from the coach? A servant of your employers, perhaps?"

"Of course," she answered swiftly, glad that he'd dropped a solution to her problem of getting rid of him into her lap.

Her heart twisted a little at the idea of getting rid of him and thus never seeing him again. But she ignored that because the heart, she now realised, was a foolish organ.

Look at Christopher. His feelings for Althea Furberg had completely blinded him to the woman's machinations.

And whilst Lydia and Alex had worked things out, the start of their relationship had been anything but smooth.

Besides, even if she *was* interested in Mr. Lauer, she was the Crown Princess. Her father would never consent to a match with an untitled gentleman.

She thought back to the tragic tale of Aunt Anya. Harriet used to think it funny that her aunt and her mother shared a name. As a child, she hadn't noticed anything but that about her deceased aunt.

But having heard that the woman was ostracised completely for falling in love with an English aristocrat, she realised how unyielding a royal life really was. Even a princess, who could never inherit the Crown, wasn't free to make her own decisions.

And if an earl hadn't been good enough for Harriet's grandpa, who'd been king at the time of Aunt Anya's marriage, then a mere gentleman could never be good enough for Father.

"Miss Royal?"

Harriet started as she realised that he'd been talking to her while she'd been wool-gathering, imagining herself marrying him, for goodness sake! She barely knew him and didn't even like him half the time.

"I'm sorry, I didn't quite catch that."

He smiled, and Harriet's stomach dipped in reaction.

"I said, I'll be glad to meet the person sent to escort you onward, Miss Royal. It will put my mind at ease."

With another grin, he leaned back against the cushioned bench and closed his eyes.

Well, Harriet thought, *drat.*

SHE WAS COMMITTED to her lies, that much could be said for her.

Jacob inwardly laughed as he wondered what nonsense she'd come up with to explain her lack of escort when they got to Gant.

He questioned briefly if he should be enjoying himself this much. After all, this was just another job. One he needed expedited so he could return to the palace and do some real work.

Being a spy had no glory, no offers of titles or lands as payment for service. But it was lucrative. And Jacob enjoyed it. Enjoyed the danger, the excitement, the freedom.

Which was why this nannying would fast grow boring. He was sure of it.

And much as he'd rather surprisingly enjoyed the company of Princess Harriet and was vastly amused at her attempts of subterfuge, he knew it could only be a day or two before he grew irritated at playing nursemaid to the girl.

He heard her sigh, and she wriggled in the seat, her leg pressing against his own, and Jacob found himself gritting his teeth against a surge of desire.

That was another thing.

The attraction he felt was more than inconvenient. It was downright dangerous. So, the sooner he could put some distance between himself and the princess, the better.

The carriage rattled and bumped its way along the road as Jacob gave the impression that he was sleeping.

In truth, he was very much awake and aware of everything. He'd been aware of the man who tried to get into the seat beside the princess. And aware of the other man whose eyes were alert and hostile, leading Jacob to believe he was an opportunistic thief.

And he was all too aware of the floral, springtime scent that surrounded the princess, just as he was all too aware of the way her dark, almost sable curls had loosened as the day wore on, with some now falling to brush against her shoulders. Aware, too, of the flecks of bronze in her wide, brown eyes.

Jacob's thoughts screeched to a halt as he felt the sudden drop of a head to his shoulder, and his senses were overwhelmed with that floral scent that had been driving him to distraction.

His eyes snapped open and he looked down as much as he could without disturbing her. He saw nothing past the monstrosity of a bonnet that she wore in an effort to disguise herself.

But the simple action of putting her head on his shoulder affected Jacob in ways that shocked him.

The overwhelming feeling of protectiveness that

surged within him went beyond mere duty to his assignment, and even to the Crown.

It was all about the woman on his shoulder, and wanting, nay needing her to be safe.

His blood ran cold as he thought for the hundredth time of what could have befallen her had she taken this journey alone.

Still, she wasn't alone, he reminded himself as his heartbeat picked up in the oddest way.

He was here. And he was determined that she'd be safe. From her own impulsiveness as well as from whatever or whoever was threatening the royal family.

The carriage hit a bump, and Harriet jolted slightly but instead of waking, she merely sighed and snuggled closer into his shoulder.

Jacob swallowed past a sudden lump in his throat as his heartbeat skittered even more.

And he knew, if he wasn't careful, he could be in trouble.

Chapter Seven

***

HARRIET SLOWLY BECAME aware of a bright light behind her eyelids, of unfamiliar sounds surrounding her. For a moment, she forgot where she was.

Where was her satin pillow? Where was her soft, luxurious bedding? And what on earth was that wonderful smell?

She turned her head into the warm, smooth skin pressed against her lips and inhaled deeply, relishing the feel of the corded muscles at her mouth.

Her stomach knotted as desire, potent and unfamiliar, heated her veins.

She was just getting ready to push herself closer to the rock-solid warmth pressed against her when a door by the side of her was thrown wide and a shout rent the air.

Harriet bolted upright, the haze of sleep departing and reality swooping in. And with it, the knowledge that she had just been sniffing the neck of Mr. Lauer.

Harriet felt her cheeks scald with shame, and she refused, simply refused to look at him.

"Good morning, Miss Royal."

His voice sounded brightly beside her, the trace of amusement evident. "I trust you slept well?"

"Uh – thank you, yes," she stammered, acutely aware that she'd awoken not only with her mouth pressed against his neck, but the rest of her snuggled into him, too. For shame!

"Good. Well, I think we need to get you out of the coach and fed as soon as possible."

His words made so little sense that she frowned up at him in confusion.

"Fed?" she asked, wondering if her stomach had been grumbling loudly, causing even further embarrassment.

"Indeed," he answered gravely, his blue eyes boring into her own. "After all, if the door hadn't opened when it did, I'm quite certain you would have eaten me alive. I was in fear for my life, Miss Royal. Or at least my neck. Clearly, it smelled good to you."

Harriet felt her mouth drop open as unequivocal shame swept through her, bringing with it a healthy measure of anger. At herself for acting thus, and at the blighter now grinning wickedly down at her for being ill-mannered enough to bring it up.

"I didn't – I wasn't—" She was so embarrassed she

could barely get the words out.

"Don't trouble yourself, Miss Royal. I rather enjoyed the experience."

Harriet opened her mouth to deliver a scathing set down. But she couldn't find the words. She could barely even see past the red mist of anger and embarrassment.

Opening and closing her mouth like a demented fish, she finally settled on a strangled sort of scream of frustration before turning her head away from his amused smirk and scrambling out of the conveyance.

She didn't bother waiting for any sort of assistance, since someone had already placed a step at the door.

Harriet stood fuming whilst the driver and coachmen removed the luggage from the top of the coach, throwing them, rather haphazardly to her mind, on the muddy road below.

She kept herself rigidly still, her mortification, exhaustion, and hunger all vying for first place in her turbulent thoughts.

How *dare* he? He was a cad. A blackguard. A scoundrel!

Harriet's bags suddenly hit the ground at her feet with a thump, and she immediately moved to retrieve them.

Her muscles screamed in protest, sore from a bumpy night trussed up against that awful man, but she didn't care. She'd rather *die* than let him offer any sort of assistance.

She couldn't believe she'd ever thought him gentlemanly or charming.

Harriet bent and hefted one of her bags. Straightening back up, she almost toppled over with the weight of it, but she managed to stay upright, even if she staggered a bit.

Huffing out a breath, she eyed the next bag, trying to figure out just how she'd manage it.

She looked hopefully at the men who'd worked on the coach, but they'd finished throwing luggage on the ground and were even now moving off toward the stables of the inn.

Harriet wondered fleetingly where Mr. Lauer had gone, but she absolutely refused to turn around to look for him.

"Right." She took a deep breath, shifted her bag to one hand then leaned down to pick up the next.

The heavy bag she held swung forward, and she had to drop it lest she fall into the muck.

Harriet threw her eyes heavenward, praying for patience.

She was starting to sweat from her efforts and the bright morning sun beating down on her back.

"Come on, Harriet," she mumbled to herself. "You can do this."

With renewed determination, she flung back the material of her cloak, pushed up the sleeves of her simple muslin gown and bent forward to clap both bags.

With a very unladylike grunt, she heaved the bags up, managing to lift them both a few inches off the ground.

She thought longingly of the small gig she'd stolen from the palace grounds so she didn't have to carry her bags before abandoning it near the public coach.

She felt as though her arms would fall off with the weight of the bags, but at least she was carrying them.

Taking a huge breath, Harriet turned—and smacked straight into a solid wall. A warm, rather nice smelling solid wall.

She gasped aloud, the bags dropping to her feet. She would have fallen backwards onto the dirt if a large pair of hands hadn't shot out and grabbed her.

"*What* are you doing?" she demanded through gritted teeth, her annoyance at his earlier teasing, coupled with her annoyance that he'd made her drop her hard won luggage, making her more than a little grouchy.

"I wondered if I might be of assistance, Miss Royal?"

He was all politeness and charm. But she wasn't fooled by it. The man was a veritable cad, teasing her and flirting with her and making her heart beat inexplicably fast.

"No, thank you," she answered as primly as she

could considering he still held her, his big, overgrown hands searing her even through the material of her gown.

The cloak was still flung over her shoulders in a ridiculous fashion. Her skin was burning, her eyes were stinging, and she was feeling more than a little overwhelmed.

Harriet found herself wishing for a moment that Christopher had sent someone charging after her. If she were to be dragged back to the luxury of the palace, she could protest quite vocally about it and pretend she wasn't secretly pleased.

But she was committed now and truth be told, Harriet didn't think she could face another journey like the one she'd just taken so soon. Especially not alone.

"Remove your hands from me at once," she bit out, aware that she couldn't have sounded haughtier if she tried.

Mr. Lauer immediately removed his hands, holding them up in a manner that was probably intended to placate her but merely served to anger her further.

How dare he stand there with his hands up as though *she* were the one being unreasonable?

"Your companion doesn't seem to have made an appearance, Miss Royal." He dropped his hands and stepped forward, forcing her to stumble back, tripping over one of her loathsome bags.

"And?" she huffed.

In truth, Harriet had never been so unfriendly, nor so ill-tempered.

But there was just something about the handsome stranger that set her on edge.

And she was more than a little embarrassed at having *sniffed* the man.

"And as I said when you sniffed me—" He grinned now as though he'd known where her mind had wandered. "I feel that I should at least see that you're fed while you're waiting. Perhaps he, or she, is delayed?"

Harriet's temper flared again.

"Mind your own damned business," she spat before she could stop the words. She clamped a hand over her mouth, but of course, it wasn't as though she could put the words back in.

Never before had she cursed. She was the Crown Princess, for goodness sake! This – this *cad* brought out the very worst in her.

As she stared at him in horror, a grin suddenly broke out across his face and those dimples made an appearance. Despite her hatred of the man, Harriet's heart still stuttered at the sight and that just made her even more annoyed.

Pointedly turning her back on him, she bent down and hefted the bags. Her mortification lent her a strength she didn't know she had, and she managed to get them both off the ground without falling over.

With as much dignity as she could manage, Harriet tilted her chin and marched off, away from him and his arrogance, and his dimples.

Her march lasted a couple of seconds before the weight of the bags began to take effect, but Harriet would rather *die* than stop or put them down while he was watching.

So, on she went. At more of a shuffle than a walk. But at least she was doing it alone, without any help.

And, she told herself with a spurt of pride, she'd managed to get away from the palace and to Gant all alone without interference.

It felt good to be independent. And she wasn't going to let Christopher, or Alex, or that awful Mr. Lauer stop her.

Chapter Eight

ONCE AGAIN, JACOB found himself torn between amusement and frustration as he watched Princess Harriet shuffle away like an eighty-year-old woman.

She had gumption; he'd give her that. And he hadn't expected it from her.

In truth, he hadn't expected any sort of personality at all. In his experience, women of the upper echelons of Society were banal in the extreme. And Princess Harriet was literally their leader.

But he'd been wrong. She had more personalities than he knew what to do with, in point of fact. And at the moment, she was a veritable shrew.

Jacob muffled an oath as she staggered away then laughed softly as his own swearing reminded him of hers.

The perfect princess with the muck mouth.

He shouldn't have riled her up like that—teasing

her the way he had.

But he hadn't been able to help himself. For some reason, he thrived on getting a reaction from the princess.

And teasing her had been a sure fire way to get her het up and away from him. Something he'd definitely needed to do at the time.

Truthfully, as inconvenient and unwelcome as it was having her lying against him so trustingly then feeling those lips pressed to his skin, it had awoken a desire in Jacob that he'd never felt before. There was no escaping it, and no getting around it.

And God help him, he knew that if he'd stayed there, with her pressed against him like that, and her lips tantalisingly close, he'd have kissed her.

It had gotten her away from him well enough. And given him some much-needed space to get his body back under control.

But it had backfired, too.

Jacob hadn't accounted for the woman's sheer stubbornness, and now he had to think on his feet again.

How was it that a nannying job had caused him more hassle in twenty-four hours than any of his other jobs did in weeks?

He watched worriedly as she stumbled before righting herself. He'd carried those bags. They were manageable but heavy, and the princess was positively tiny compared to him. She wouldn't get far with the weight of them.

And Jacob couldn't even allow himself to think of the trouble she could get herself into alone on the road like that.

The Winter Palace was a goodly walk away, even without luggage. She'd never bloody make it!

As he watched, one of the bags fell from her grip, and he laughed aloud as she kicked the offending item before bending to retrieve it.

His mouth dried at the view and he turned away quickly.

Jacob had done a lot of stupid things in his time but lusting after the Crown Princess of Aldonia was bad, even for him.

He gave his head a shake, refocusing himself.

The job here was to keep the princess safe until she gave up on this ridiculous exercise and went home. Then he could get back to his real life and the investigation into the assassination attempt.

That meant he had to stop being amused by her temper, or charmed by her wide-eyed innocence, or attracted to any part of her.

Ignoring the ridiculous surge of protectiveness he felt around her, Jacob turned back toward the inn.

If he was going to carry out this assignment correctly, he needed to give her a head start.

Even if he didn't want to.

Jacob walked toward the inn, his mind filled with hastily made plans. If she gave up as quickly as he hoped, they could be back at the palace within a couple of days.

For now, he'd eat and find a conveyance of some sort.

His stomach churned uneasily as he imagined Princess Harriet on the road alone and struggling, but he ruthlessly ignored it.

She was a job. Just a job.

INDEPENDENCE WAS HIGHLY overrated, Harriet decided.

The day was far hotter than it should be for this time of year, she was sure.

The sun felt like a blazing fire beating down upon her back, and her arms felt as though they would drop off any minute.

She felt as though she'd been walking for days, and she daren't take a break lest she sit down and never stand up again.

"You can do this," she said aloud, hoping it would make the sentiment true. "This isn't difficult. You *wanted* this," she reminded herself.

Her stomach rumbled, and her throat was parched. Her feet were hurting, and she could almost guarantee that her toes were blistered.

Harriet glanced up at the sun and was dismayed to see that it hadn't even moved. It felt as though she'd been walking all day. The truth was it had probably only been a couple of hours.

She felt pathetic tears spring to her eyes but refused to let them fall. What sort of adventuress cried because her feet hurt, for goodness sake?

The distant sound of horses' hooves caught Harriet's attention, and she spun around to look hopefully down the road.

If someone could offer her assistance, could get her closer to her destination, she would be eternally grateful.

And she would pay, of course.

She'd nearly promise someone all the jewels in the royal stores to be able to sit down and have something or someone else carry her bags for a while.

As she watched, a gig came into view, the wheels and hooves of the horse kicking up dust on the dry dirt road.

The sun prevented Harriet from being able to see clearly, but there was a lone occupant and it was obviously a man. A big one, too.

Once again, Harriet found herself with a difficult decision to make. It wasn't safe, she knew it wasn't safe, to travel alone with a strange man. Yet she'd never get anywhere at this pace, and the daylight wouldn't last forever.

She squinted against the bright sunlight but couldn't make out anything about the man other than the sheer size of him.

As the conveyance came closer, Harriet made a snap decision and dropped the bags so she could wave the driver down.

The truth was that she wasn't going to get anywhere near her destination on foot, and the road alone in the middle of the night, surrounded by deep, dark forest, was sure to be far more dangerous than travelling with a man who could be a kindly farmer, or even a vicar.

Harriet felt her spirits rise as she reminded herself that she was far more likely to meet someone kind and pleasant than a would-be murderer.

Her mood immediately lightened at the prospect of a seat and not having to carry her luggage, and she stepped more fully onto the road and prepared to get the driver's attention.

Before she lifted her arm however, she studied the form of the driver more closely.

There was something familiar about the set of his shoulders. A niggling familiarity.

As she studied him, a frown of concentration marring her brow, a dawning horror awakened in her.

"Oh, no," she whispered.

Every expletive she'd ever heard Christopher and Alex express tumbled around in her head.

She considered running but it was too late. In any case, running was out of the question with those blasted bags.

While Harriet stood there wringing her hands over what to do, the gig drew to a stop.

"Miss Royal, we meet again."

Harriet gritted her teeth as she looked into the smugly grinning face of Mr. Lauer.

Chapter Nine

~•~

THE SCOWL ON Princess Harriet's face could have curdled milk, and Jacob found himself grinning like a dolt.

He had no idea why her irritation with him amused him so.

He studied her as she stood there, hands placed firmly on her hips, riotous sable curls escaping the confines of the oversized bonnet.

"What are you doing here?" she bit out, the chocolate depths of her eyes sparkling with ill-concealed annoyance.

"Why, I'm driving my gig, Miss Royal. What are *you* doing? Where is your companion?"

He arranged his features to show polite concern and nothing more.

"He – she – um—"

Jacob watched her flounder for a moment or two before he took pity.

She really was dreadful at this.

"Perhaps there was a delay in sending the servant to you?"

Her eyes widened.

"Yes!" She dove on the proffered excuse. "Yes, that's exactly it."

"Well then, allow me to drive you to wherever you are going, Miss Royal."

"Oh, um, I'd rather—"

"Miss Royal," he interrupted her before she started throwing around poor excuses. "It's hot, and I've felt for myself how heavy those bags are. Please, allow me to assist you in this. I can drive you to your destination, and you'll never have to see me again."

He watched as she contemplated his words, chewing her lip in a way he was determined not to be distracted by.

Jacob had waited in the inn baffled by his level of concern for the princess before he'd decided two hours was enough time so that it could reasonably be a coincidence to meet her on the road.

He'd spent far too much money obtaining this gig and gelding from a drunken farmer before setting out after her.

The entire way, he'd berated himself for his over-inflated sense of worry about the girl. But, he had been relieved to reason; it was his job, after all. The prince wanted his sister safe, and wanted Jacob to be the one to keep her safe. That was all. He'd been happy, too, with such reasoning, confident that it was attention to the detail of the job, and nothing more that was causing this unusual worry.

Then he'd spied her struggling along the road, and his heart had squeezed in the most unusual and disconcerting manner.

She looked tiny and vulnerable even now when she was glaring at him.

And even though the entire assignment was anathema to Jacob, he couldn't help but have a grudging admiration for the lady's spirit.

Still, now was not the time to be admiring any part of her.

"You can't," she blurted, dragging his mind back to the matter at hand.

"Why not?" he asked.

"Where I'm going is – um – out of the way."

Ah. Jacob realised she couldn't very well ask him to drop her off at her palace.

Again, he wondered at her complete inability to put together any sort of reasonable, workable plan, and he found himself actually feeling *grateful* for Prince Christopher having the sagacity to have engaged Jacob's help.

Though he'd have preferred the job to have been someone else's. Especially when she was glaring at him like that.

He pretended to consider her words before hopping down from the gig so he could stand in front of her.

Her face was flushed. He'd guess from the exertion of dragging her luggage up the road. And probably from the hatred she felt within when looking at him.

"I don't mind driving out of the way if it means you are safe, Miss Royal," he said. And he meant it. He'd drive her all the way back home right now if it kept her safe.

Princess Harriet stared at her bags for an age.

"W-well, I—" She stumbled to a halt then suddenly lifted her gaze to meet his own, and damned if his heart didn't stutter as her huge brown eyes met his.

And Jacob felt sorry for her. She was in over her head, and she looked fed up and worn out.

It was all well and good trying to catch her out, but standing here arguing whilst she was dead on her feet wasn't exactly taking care of her.

"Perhaps as a compromise I could at least bring you closer to wherever your destination is?" he asked, watching her face carefully, whilst she did the same.

It was obvious that the princess was hesitant about trusting him, yet she seemed to believe all of his subterfuges easily enough.

She was naïve. Innocent and unused to the real world. And that's why the world was so dangerous for her.

Even ignoring the possible threat to her life.

"I'm heading in the direction of the Winter Palace," he announced, once more checking her reactions.

As he'd suspected, her face gave her away.

Her eyes widened, and for a moment they filled with a relief that would have given her away to an amateur.

"Oh, um. That is – that is quite close to where I'm staying." She tried to sound casual, but he wasn't fooled. She was practically salivating as she eyed the carriage.

He could practically see the cogs in her brain turning. He could only imagine that she was torn between giving away her location and being stranded here on the side of the road.

"Then allow me to take you at least as far as there, Miss Royal," he said smoothly, keeping his tone clear of any inflection.

She eyed him closely for a moment, and Jacob felt a sudden bout of nervousness.

If she refused his help, he wouldn't have a lot of options left. Kidnapping her seemed extreme.

"Very well," she finally answered to his relief. "But only as far as the outer wall of the gardens," she insisted. "I can manage from there."

Jacob felt a surge of relief but kept his face smooth as he nodded his agreement.

Then, before she could argue any more about anything else, he bent and plucked her bags from the ground, stowing them on the floor of the conveyance.

"I'm afraid that it will be quite a squeeze for our feet, Miss Royal," he said apologetically. "I don't have enough rope to secure your luggage to the back."

"That's quite all right," she answered, and he could hear the relief in her tone. "Anything is better than carrying them."

Jacob turned back toward her and his heart flipped, taking him by surprise.

She looked completely exhausted.

Without any real conscious thought, he stepped forward and swept her into his arms.

Princess Harriet's gasp of shock had no effect on him.

Nor did her outraged protests.

When her arms wrapped around his neck to balance herself, however, he found himself more than a little affected.

And even though her eyes were shooting daggers at him and loathing was coming off her in waves, he couldn't seem to tamp down the flame of desire licking along his veins.

"Unhand me, you brute," she bit out, her hands clasping his greatcoat in a vicelike grip. "How dare you pick me up without permission? Without *warning*."

Jacob ignored her ramblings and deposited her none-too-gently in the seat of the gig.

A part of him might find her desirable, but the rest of him had the sense to just find her irritating.

Sending a prayer heavenward for patience, Jacob climbed into the carriage beside her, taking the reins and offering a conciliatory smile.

"Shall we?" he asked.

Princess Harriet eyed him, singularly unimpressed with his attempts to charm.

"I suppose we must," she sniffed and turned her face away before she could see his scowl.

This was going to be a long journey.

HARRIET WANTED TO weep with the relief of sitting down, resting her feet, and having her bags transported for her.

She wouldn't show it, however.

She wouldn't give him the satisfaction of knowing he'd rescued her from a serious predicament.

Harriet had no idea why he affected her so. And she didn't care to find out.

All she knew was that she felt constantly discomfited in his company.

That he'd embarrassed, and infuriated, and annoyed her more in the last twenty-four hours than anyone in her life before.

And that, to her shame and confusion, when he'd

lifted her into his arms as though she weighed no more than a feather, her stomach had twisted with the most alarming bolt of desire, and it had been all Harriet could do to stop herself from pressing her lips to his own.

Which was decidedly *not* what she should be feeling.

"Are you hungry, Miss Royal?"

The softly spoken question interrupted Harriet's confusing thoughts, and as though reminded by his question, her stomach rumbled.

Harriet's cheeks flushed as he grinned then leaned over one of the bags that had been squashed into the seat between them. The other was at Harriet's feet. Not entirely comfortable, but she wasn't about to complain when the alternative had been walking and carrying it.

"Here, I did notice you didn't break your fast."

She looked down to see a bundle wrapped in a clean, linen cloth.

"It's not much," he said. "But it will stop you from swooning on me."

Harriet snorted in a most unladylike fashion even as she took the bundle from his hands.

"I don't swoon," she answered. "And I can't imagine someone like you having a problem with a lady swooning at his feet, in any case."

"Someone like me," he repeated with a small smile. "You have me all figured out, hmm? Well, you're not wrong. I enjoy a good swoon as much as the next red-blooded male."

Harriet rolled her eyes and opened the bundle, almost crying at the sight of freshly baked bread and a lump of cheese. There was even a ripe plum, which would help quench her thirst. He was resourceful, she admitted grudgingly to herself. And thoughtful, too.

"But when a lady swoons over me, I'd much rather it be because of my devilish good looks and charm. Not because she's unconscious from hunger."

"You have an extremely high opinion of yourself, Mr. Lauer. Has anyone ever told you that?"

"Frequently." He grinned unabashedly, and Harriet had to bite the inside of her mouth to keep from laughing. She refused to encourage him. "But you're the only one who's ever made me feel as though it was undeserved."

This time she couldn't hold in her giggle. He was incorrigible.

And he had rescued her, she admitted. More than once.

"Thank you," she said softly. "For the food and – and everything else."

His piercing blue eyes softened as they raked over her face, and Harriet's throat tightened, though she couldn't have said why.

"You're welcome," he said softly, sincerely.

And they lapsed into a silence that felt more comfortable than it should.

Chapter Ten

"$\mathcal{A}$s I said before, Mr. Lauer, I thank you for your offer, but it really isn't necessary."

Jacob was rather impressed with himself that he could understand every word she spoke through teeth as gritted as hers currently were.

They'd been arguing for almost an hour now, and if she didn't start cooperating, it would be pitch black before he got her to see any sense.

He thought longingly of the time he'd been captured in Berlin and had to endure beatings and interrogations for three weeks before he and Hans had escaped.

At the time, he'd thought that a terrible situation to be in. He'd kill for the dank, dark cell and a bit of physical torture right now. It had been a veritable holiday compared to arguing with the little hoyden in front of him.

"You said you'd just drop me where I wanted to

go," Princess Harriet continued, glaring at him.

"And you said somebody would be meeting you here," he pointed out reasonably. Here being a two-mile walk from the gates of the Winter Palace. This was nothing more than a densely populated forest.

Surely the girl didn't mean to camp out!

Princess Harriet threw her hands in the air as if he were the one being bloody impossible.

What he wanted was for her to trust him enough to tell him where she planned to go, and what she planned to do.

He'd hoped that feeding her would improve her mood, and he supposed it had. Somewhat.

But damn it all, she was right back to being a recalcitrant little shrew.

"Well, I lied," she bit out defiantly. "There is nobody coming to meet me. I am travelling onward alone."

Jacob couldn't be sure if her admission was progress or not.

One thing he was absolutely sure about however was that she was going nowhere alone.

"Then let me *help* you," he said for the hundredth time.

"No," she answered mutinously for the hundredth time.

And so, they stood here at in impasse glaring at each other like combatants across a battlefield.

"Why are you alone?" he suddenly blurted, hoping that she'd be honest now that she was shouting the truth at him.

She rolled her eyes heavenward, quite clearly fed up of him.

Heaving a sigh, her big, brown gaze met his own and his heart stuttered.

He didn't have time to be distracted by her beauty.

He didn't have a damned clue what to do with the surge of intense emotion that look from those eyes inspired. Something he'd never experienced before—a confusing mix of desire and protectiveness.

Whatever it was, it had no place here.

"I needed a break from – from my family. My life."

He noticed immediately that she'd slipped up. Back at the inn, she'd claimed her family was dead. Further proof that she was a terrible liar. His frown of confusion was genuine.

What could a Crown Princess want a break from? She lived a gilded existence. Spoiled by her brothers and parents, adored by her subjects, admired by dignitaries and aristocrats the world over.

"They are alive then, your family?" he asked, and watched her eyes widen in dismay as she obviously realised she'd been caught out.

Her sigh sounded as though it came from the depths of her soul.

"Yes, they're alive," she mumbled.

"Do they—" he began, not sure how to phrase a question he really didn't want to ask. "Are they cruel?" Prince Christopher didn't seem as though he would hurt his sister, but Jacob supposed one never knew what happened behind closed doors.

If anyone, royal or otherwise, abused her in some way, that changed things. He wouldn't bring her back to a bad situation—ordered to or not.

But to his relief, she was already shaking her head in denial.

"No, they're not cruel. Just – just protective," she hedged. "My family are – well, powerful you might say."

Yes, you might, he agreed silently. Considering they were the royal bloody family.

"And they mean well. But—" She shrugged helplessly. "My brother wants to send me away to England. And I don't want to go."

"Send you away?" he repeated. "Why?"

Jacob couldn't have said why this news displeased him so. Only that it did. He'd known that the princess was being sent with the Furbergs before she'd run. But not that she was being sent from Aldonia.

"It doesn't matter why. All that matters is that I don't want to go. And I don't want him making all of my decisions anymore."

She studied his face as though looking for a reaction, and because he didn't know what she was looking for or what might send her storming off into the forest, he kept his expression smooth.

After a while she sighed again.

"It sounds ridiculous," she muttered. "But my whole life I've never been able to go anywhere by myself, decide anything for myself, and when Christo—I mean, my brother—wanted to send me away, I thought maybe, just this once, I could strike out on my own."

Her shoulders slumped, and Jacob felt that odd protectiveness once more.

"I didn't even make it past the first day without help."

She sounded so despondent, so desolate, that Jacob's heart twisted.

"I don't know about that, Miss Royal. There isn't a single lady of my acquaintance that would have the courage to do what you've done."

He watched in fascination as a pink blush crept into her cheeks and she smiled up at him.

"And I'm sure," he continued, noting the sudden gruffness in his tone, "that had I left you to your own devices, you would have found a way to manage perfectly well without my interference."

Her smile widened, those sinful eyes sparkling with pleasure, and Jacob felt a burst of pride that he'd made her smile in such difficult circumstances.

Perhaps, he thought hopefully, she was ready to

return home. Now that someone had acknowledged her bravery, now that she'd proven she could do it—or at least thought she could do it—she'd return to safety.

"Thank you, Mr. Lauer," she said softly, and it was all Jacob could do to keep from reaching out to her.

It was getting harder and harder to remember that the princess was off limits.

"Now that you've proven you can do it, perhaps you'd like to go home?" he blurted, more harshly than he'd intended.

The second the words were out of his mouth, Jacob knew they'd been a mistake.

Her eyes hardened, her shoulders stiffened, and that defiant chin of hers notched up.

"I don't think so, Mr. Lauer," she answered glacially. "If you'll excuse me?"

He watched in amazement as she bent down, heaved up both of her silly, oversized bags, teetered around a bit under their weight, then righted herself and began to stagger off.

Jacob prayed for patience. And when that didn't work, he cursed fluently in five languages then set off chasing after the runaway princess. Again.

HARRIET FUMED HER way through the forest, not even paying attention to where she was going.

For a moment—a brief, wonderful moment, she had felt as though someone understood her. She thought that perhaps Mr. Lauer understood her need for a sense of freedom. Freedom from the strictures of her life. Freedom to make her own path, even temporarily.

There'd been something in his piercing blue eyes— a sense of affinity. But no, she was wrong. He was just another man who'd barrelled into life and wanted to control what she did. At least Christopher, Alexander, and her father were related to her. This oversized, overbearing, overly handsome man was a practical stranger.

"Miss Royal."

Harriet rolled her eyes. And he was harder to shake than the royal bloody guard.

"What?" she bit out over her shoulder. She knew she resembled a toddler having a tantrum, but she couldn't help it.

"You're going to do yourself an injury."

"Well it will be *my* injury then," she shouted back churlishly. "And *my* business."

"Please, Miss Royal. I don't want you to hurt yourself."

Harriet swung back around to glare at him as he came stomping through the trees toward her.

"Get it through your thick skull, Mr. Lauer—" She enunciated every syllable so there'd be no confusion. "I am not a child. And I will *not* hurt myself."

Hoping that finally her point had gotten across, Harriet turned back around and marched away.

Straight into the branch of a tree.

She heard an exclamation from behind her as the world tilted alarmingly.

And then, darkness descended.

JACOB DARTED THROUGH the trees, but he knew he wouldn't get to Princess Harriet in time.

He winced as her body crumpled to the forest floor.

The fear and concern that burst through him was palpable. And not just because the Crown Princess had managed to knock herself unconscious on his watch.

No, Jacob could be honest enough to admit that something in the vicinity of his heart lurched alarmingly as he heard the crack of her skull on the branch and watched helplessly as she fell.

Damn it, *why* did he have to rile her so? Why couldn't he keep his stupid mouth shut?

She was hurt.

Hurt because of him.

Jacob reached her prone body and dropped to his knees on the damp forest floor.

His heart thundered and his hands shook as he reached out to remove the ridiculous bonnet from her head.

The sight of a trickle of blood oozing beneath one of her chestnut curls nearly had Jacob casting up his accounts.

He'd had to treat his own gunshot wounds, sword injuries, even popped his own dislocated bones back into place a time or two.

Never had he felt as sick or heartsore as watching the princess's blood mar her beautiful face. And all because of him.

If Prince Christopher didn't kill him, his guilt would probably do the job.

Jacob reached out an unsteady hand and brushed the hair back from the princess's face.

Her groan of protest was the sweetest sound he'd ever heard.

As he watched closely, she slowly opened her eyes, blinked rapidly, then stared up at him.

"Are you well, Princess?" he asked softly, hoping that she hadn't seriously injured herself.

She didn't answer at first, gazing wide-eyed at him and making him feel all sorts of things he had no business feeling.

But as the silence stretched on, her eyes narrowed slightly, and Jacob realised that he'd slipped up, calling her by her title.

"You know who I am?" he pressed on before she could think overly long on it, a new set of worries clamouring for attention.

Head injuries, Jacob knew, were the most unpredictable. What if she'd forgotten him?

To his relief, she nodded slowly, wincing at even that small gesture.

"You're Mr. Lauer," she said. "The man who has caused me nothing but problems since we met."

Well, thought Jacob, *if she's well enough to bloody insult me, then she's probably well enough.*

"Can you sit up?" he asked, piously ignoring her acerbic tone.

She did so slowly, not even objecting when he wrapped a supporting arm around her.

The bonnet he'd untied stayed on the ground below her and her hair trailed down her back, a riot of sable curls littered with twigs and leaves.

She looked enchanting, like a wood nymph. She looked dangerous as hell.

Forcing himself to concentrate on her wellbeing and not on – well – *her*, Jacob removed a handkerchief and pressed it against the cut on her head, wincing right along with her.

He'd need to get her somewhere with light so he could check the damage properly. And they were miles from the Winter Palace and even further from the village.

"You're going to have quite a lump," he said softly, his eyes focused on the side of her forehead where there was a bump already forming.

"Oh, that's marvellous," she answered with a rueful grin that pleased Jacob more than he could say. No swooning and crying from the princess. "I imagine I look like a troll."

"You look beautiful," he answered before he even realised what he was doing. "Like a forest fairy."

Realising what he'd said, he met her startled gaze and watched as a delicate blush stained her cheeks.

Clearing his throat, Jacob removed the handkerchief from her head and dragged his mind back to matters at hand.

"Let's get you up," he said brusquely, all business now.

She nodded carefully again, but her eyes were watchful and they never left his face.

When she was on her feet, he let go but stayed close.

She swayed a little but her eyes were focused, a bit too focused for his comfort, and she managed to stay upright.

"Can you walk?" he asked.

"Yes, I – I think so."

"Very well. And where are we walking to?"

She opened her mouth, and Jacob just knew she was going to try to send him away.

It was time to be honest with the princess, about this at least.

"Miss Royal." He faced her and kept his expression stern so she would know that he would brook no argument. "You are hurt and alone in the middle of a forest. And I must warn you that no matter what you do or say, I am not leaving you here alone. Now, you can either trust me enough to tell me where you're heading. Or you can keep quiet and we'll stand here all night."

She opened her mouth again, but Jacob didn't give her a chance to speak.

"It's been a long couple of days. You've barely eaten, you've barely slept, and you've just lost a fight with a tree."

She scowled and he had to tamp down his amusement at her affronted expression.

"So, you can either let me help you *here,* or I can drag you back to where I found you two days ago. The choice is yours."

He crossed his arms and waited, watching one emotion after another flit across her expressive face.

She'd make a terrible spy. She wore her emotions for the world to see.

Anger, irritation, worry, confusion, uncertainty.

Ah. There it was. Grudging acceptance.

"You won't tell anyone where I am?" she mumbled quietly. Miserably. And Jacob felt that odd protectiveness well up again.

"Not a single soul," he promised. And he meant it, too. Nobody needed to know she was here. Prince Christopher only needed to know she was safe and away from whoever posed a threat to the royal family.

The princess heaved a long-suffering sigh.

"Very well," she said. "There's an old, disused woodcutter's cottage in the woods. That's where I'm going."

Jacob stared at her.

Her plan had been to stay in a rundown shack in the woods. Alone.

His gut twisted as he thought of a hundred ways danger could befall the headstrong princess if left to her own devices, but he was careful not to react, even as his heart soared with pride just a little at being taken into her confidence.

He was well aware of the leap of trust Princess Harriet had just taken by letting him in on her secret, and he didn't plan to ruin the uneasy truce by interrogating her or shaking some sense into her.

The cut on her head was still bleeding, though it was light and didn't seem to be affecting her senses. Not that she bloody had any.

But he still wanted to get her fed and warm and take care of the injury. Maybe then he'd be able to breathe properly.

"Lead the way," he said softly, picking up her bags and waiting, ensuring that no trace of his riotous emotions showed on his face.

She watched him suspiciously for a moment before finally, grudgingly, nodding her consent.

Chapter Eleven

*H*ARRIET'S NERVES WERE at a breaking point by the time the cottage's hiding place came into view.

It was so well concealed. She was sure that if circumstances had been different, she could have stayed here undiscovered.

Hidden behind a copse of dense coniferous trees and situated at the bottom of a steep hill, it wouldn't be easily spotted by anyone passing by.

Her shoulders slumped in disappointment. She'd almost gotten away with it.

Though they hadn't spoken for an age, Harriet felt Mr. Lauer's presence every step of the way.

He moved silently for someone so big, but she could feel him there nonetheless, even without the occasional nicker from the horse he led. The gig had been left in a small copse of trees by the roadside, and he had assured Harriet that nobody would find it.

Harriet's whole body was aware of his presence, and she didn't care to examine why that was.

The day had been trying enough without adding her confusing feelings about Mr. Lauer to the mix.

Like her secret relief that she wouldn't be completely alone with a head injury to contend with.

Like the fluttering in her stomach when he'd called her beautiful, or when his face had been etched with worry as he tended to the injury that was *his* fault in the first place.

Harriet could tell herself that he hadn't given her a choice about taking him into her confidence.

And he hadn't. Not really. She had no doubt he would have dragged her back home rather than leave her alone here.

But the truth was that she trusted him. Whether or not she should.

Yes, she was taking a risk, but something told her that this man was capable and inherently good. That he wouldn't hurt her or betray her trust.

And if she was wrong, well there was very little she could do about that now.

"We're here," she said quietly, feeling inexplicably shy.

They were completely alone with nobody around for miles.

Twilight had descended and the forest was becoming nothing more than shapes and shadows.

She turned to face Mr. Lauer, quite enjoying his frown of confusion.

"We are?" he asked. "Where?"

He pulled gently on the horse's reins to bring the beast to a halt.

Since the horse wasn't saddled, they'd had no choice but to walk. Mr. Lauer had wanted Harriet to sit atop the animal, but she'd been horrified enough for him to let the matter drop.

With no saddle, let alone a side saddle, and her in a carriage dress, it had been out of the question for Harriet. And when she'd pointed out the dangers of riding without a saddle through a dark forest in terrain neither she nor the horse were used to, he'd reluctantly agreed to let her walk.

Their bags, at least, were secured to the animal by the small amount of rope Mr. Lauer had found in the gig so they hadn't had to carry them. Harriet was almost on her knees with exhaustion. Having to carry anything, even Mr. Lauer's smaller valise, would have tipped her over the edge.

Her head pounded and her stomach felt sick.

She needed to lie down. But she'd die before admitting any weakness to her unwanted companion.

Instead of answering him, Harriet moved toward the clearing, knowing where the trail through the densely packed trees was.

Within minutes, the cottage came into view.

It was old and ramshackle, there was no doubt about it. And Harriet knew it wouldn't be in any sort of good repair.

But still. Since childhood, it had felt like hers. A place where she didn't have to be Princess Harriet. She could just be an ordinary girl living an ordinary life, free from the strictures she'd been born to.

Harriet was pleasantly surprised to see that the roof and windows were still mostly intact. There were holes in the thatch that she could see even from here, but no glass missing and nothing so bad as to make it unusable.

Over the years, she'd wondered if her little shack would crumble completely during the adverse weather Aldonia got during winter months.

But every time she came back here, she found it was still standing. And it always gave her a little burst of pleasure to find it so.

Usually, it was covered in feet of snow when she visited. She would stomp her way to the door and set about building a fire in the old stone grate. And then she would just sit for hours, enjoying the solitude. Reading tawdry novels. Eating the repast she always packed. Heating water by the fire and drinking tea and just being in charge of herself, if only for snippets of time.

She'd never seen it in the Spring.

And she'd never shared it with another person

before.

Perhaps that's why she felt so inexplicably on edge. That and the fact that she was alone in the middle of the woods with a man she'd only met two days prior.

"It's certainly well hidden."

Mr. Lauer's wry tone brought Harriet's mind back to the present. And her present predicament.

How long did he plan on staying with her? Surely he couldn't expect to stay the night?

Yet trying to send him away again was futile, she knew.

He was as stubborn as an ox and would refuse to leave her, in any case.

He probably assumed that a lady who would run away from a respectable family all alone was the type of lady with loose morals who wouldn't care about spending nights alone with a man.

But he couldn't be more wrong!

Harriet didn't want this experience to *ruin* her reputation.

And whilst it wouldn't do her too much damage considering she was the Crown Princess, she still didn't want people thinking such things of her.

The crown would make her a desirable match, no matter what she did. Which was part of the reason for her running, she supposed. Being seen as a crown and not a person took its toll.

"Shall we, Miss Royal?"

Harriet was torn between wanting him to disappear and wanting him to stay.

Her head was pounding enough to make her feel quite nauseated. Her stomach was growling. She was cold, and tired, and—though she was loathe to admit it—rather scared.

Perhaps his company wouldn't be so bad. He didn't seem dangerous.

It was just that her heart had that annoying habit of picking up speed when he was around.

"Miss Royal?"

Harriet didn't trust herself to speak at that particular moment, so she just took a step forward, leading the way inside her sanctuary and hoping she wasn't making a colossal mistake.

JACOB WATCHED CAREFULLY as Princess Harriet staggered slightly.

He felt like a fussing mother hen, but he couldn't help it. She was fit to drop, even aside from her head injury.

Her hiding place had surprised him. He didn't think a precious princess would stay in such a slum, though it was in good repair.

Someone had maintained it over the years, but he doubted it was the princess.

He could tell she was nervous and oddly, he felt a similar anxiety stir inside him.

He couldn't even begin to imagine why, so instead of worrying about it, he just ignored it.

Princess Harriet pushed at the warped wooden door, which unsurprisingly didn't give.

She darted a quick glance at him and he could see, even in the dwindling daylight, that her pupils were huge, the deep brown irises almost as dark. And her eyes were glassier than he was comfortable with.

It could be exhaustion. But what if it wasn't?

Jacob's anxiety kicked up a notch and he stepped forward.

"Allow me," he said, not giving her the chance to argue because he was sure that she would.

A solid shove had the door giving way and Jacob stepped into the sparse, one-room cottage ahead of the princess, planning to chase away any scurrying creature that might frighten her.

The place, he was pleased to see, was in much better shape than he'd expected.

It was a bit dusty and slightly damp but not covered in feet of dust and grim as he'd worried it might be.

It wouldn't take him half so long to make the princess comfortable now.

His eyes darted around the room, taking everything in.

There was a simple wooden cot in the corner with

some blankets folded neatly in a pile at the end of the mattress, two rickety looking wooden chairs by the empty stone fireplace, with an even less stable looking table between them.

In the corner was a chest on which sat a teapot, two chipped mugs, and a motley collection of plates and bowls. Jacob moved to put the bags down by the chest.

He heard Princess Harriet step inside the cottage behind him, and he turned to face her.

"It's not the worst place I've ever stayed." He smiled, watching her closely. "However did you find such a place, Miss Royal?"

"Oh!" Even in the dark he could see her blush. "My – er – my family live, I mean lived, I mean – used to live close by. To here. Not too close."

Jacob hid his smirk at her fumbling.

"And – and I came here as a girl. Nobody ever seemed to live in it or even know about it. So, I sort of adopted it. It's my safe haven. Somewhere I can just – be myself."

Jacob nodded as pieces of the puzzle fell into place.

It made sense now that the cottage was in decent enough repair. Princess Harriet probably thought this place was a secret. But Jacob guessed that Prince Christopher knew about it, as did the king, and both had made sure it was maintained and safe for the princess.

He felt sorry for the princess, thinking that she had

a secret place. Her innocence surprised Jacob. Surely, she didn't think that she went anywhere or did anything without the king knowing about it. It was so naïve for one so feisty. Perhaps that was why he found the lady so distractingly intriguing.

His heart twisted as he watched her eyes light with pride as they scanned the room.

Her father or brother, perhaps both, had obviously left the place alone enough for Princess Harriet to believe it was unknown to them.

For some reason, he felt a spurt of anger toward the royal family. He didn't like the idea of them tricking her.

But isn't that what you're doing?

Jacob ignored the question rattling around his head. He was following orders. That wasn't the same thing as allowing her to think she had a secret hiding place.

Besides, he didn't have time to worry about silly emotions like guilt. He had a job to do. He needed to keep the princess safe from harm until the danger to the royal family had passed.

Or until she gave up on this ridiculous scheme and returned to the safety of the palace and the royal guard.

And letting her walk into a tree hadn't been a good way to do that, he reminded himself fiercely.

"Let me start a fire," he said evenly as his sharp eyes took in the wringing of her hands, the stiffness in her shoulders.

"Oh, that's quite all right," she answered, her smile as brittle as her faux-breezy tone. "I shan't keep you any longer, Mr. Lauer. You've been so very helpful. But I can manage from here."

He knew that she knew he wasn't going to leave. Could tell by the hopeful light in her gaze, the defiant tilt of her chin. She was preparing for battle. He was starting to recognise the signs.

"We both know I'm not leaving, Miss Royal." He tried to sound firm but unthreatening. "So, why don't I make a fire and you can empty those bags, try to find something clean that I can tend to your head wound with."

The wringing of her hands stopped.

"I hardly think that's necessary. Tis just a scratch."

Jacob sighed, making sure she knew how tedious he found her arguments. By the narrowing of her eyes, he'd guess that he'd conveyed his opinion rather well.

"Let's not go through all of this again," he said. "I'm not discussing or arguing about anything else until you're comfortable and that wound is taken care of."

"And then?" she asked with quite insulting hope.

"And then—" Jacob couldn't resist a teasing grin. "We'll get ourselves all cosy and settled down for the night."

Chapter Twelve

———❦———

$\mathcal{A}$T LEAST HER voice wasn't shrill when she was angry, Jacob mused as he collected water from the stream that ran behind the cottage.

He didn't think his ears could take her blistering if she had begun screeching.

There was no denying she was furious at his high-handedness.

He could handle her temper. Harder to handle was his bizarre attraction to it.

He'd escaped to get water, as much to let his ardour cool as her temper.

Dipping the bowl into the icy stream, Jacob contemplated throwing himself in there for good measure.

But, no.

Beautiful she may be. Spirited and courageous. But she was also spoilt, and argumentative, and unreasonable.

He didn't need cold water to take the edge off his

inexplicable desire for her. Her personality was sure to do that for him.

Feeling much more level-headed, he went back inside, grateful that the princess was where he'd instructed her to stay.

It wouldn't have surprised him if she'd made a run for it.

But as he raked his gaze over her diminutive form huddled on the cot, Jacob realised that she was likely too exhausted to run anywhere.

Her cheeks were pale and her eyes glassy.

A spurt of guilt shook him, and Jacob knew he should go easier on the princess.

A strange man, a giant compared to her, had imposed himself on her in an isolated cottage miles from her home and her family.

Jacob knew he wouldn't ever harm her, but the princess didn't know that—though he suspected that she trusted him, though likely begrudgingly.

She'd done as he had asked, at least, and he was pleased to see that she'd had the foresight to pack up some linen strips for her trip. They were laid out neatly beside her.

Her hair was tumbling down her back, the pins having been lost to the arduous journey, he'd imagine.

Jacob felt his throat dry as he watched the flames from the fire send light dancing over the sable curls, making them appear almost navy-blue at times.

He'd never seen hair as dark nor as luxurious. And his fingers itched to run through the tresses to see if they felt as silky as they looked.

Clearing his throat, he moved to the fire to heat the water, aware that he'd been gaping at her like a schoolboy with an infatuation.

"I don't suppose you have food in there?" He nodded toward the bag that she hadn't yet opened, sitting beside the one that she'd rummaged in for the bandages.

To his surprise, her face lit with a triumphant grin.

"I'm not completely without my senses, Mr. Lauer," she said, and he was relieved that she'd lost some of that wide-eyed distrust that she'd been glaring at him with since he'd announced that he was staying at the cottage.

She'd ranted and raved, even while he'd moved her bodily to the cot and told her to sit.

It was only when he'd assured her that he'd sleep outside with the horse if it made her feel more comfortable that she'd finally settled down.

That, and the fact that she'd begun swaying alarmingly.

He answered her grin with one of his own. A truce was better than a war, after all.

"May I?" he asked and when she nodded, he lifted the bag and brought it to the table at the hearth.

Jacob's eyes widened as he opened the valise and

took in the contents.

There were breads, cheeses, cured meats. One pot contained tea leaves. Another, an assortment of biscuits and little pastries.

"I have a bit of a sweet tooth," she confessed with a charming blush.

Jacob's eyes watched the trail of pink start at her throat and move slowly to her cheeks.

Stop it, he told himself sternly.

Moving his eyes back to the contents of the bag, Jacob frowned slightly.

There was enough for two, maybe three days.

His guess was that she wouldn't go shopping in the little hamlet the coach had arrived in.

And she didn't seem like she was planning on going home any time soon.

"You know there isn't enough to feed you here for long? The food you've brought will spoil easily, if it hasn't already."

"I know that," she snapped, and he realised she was annoyed again.

Perhaps she was just hungry.

Without another word, Jacob set about preparing a meal while he waited for the water on the fire to boil.

When it started to bubble, he made tea for both of them, even though he despised the stuff, then poured the remaining water into a clean bowl.

"Can you sit by the fire?" he asked, aware that she'd

watched him in complete silence.

Wordlessly, she stood and grabbed the linens, then moved to take the seat across from him.

"It's easier to see by the firelight," he explained, even though she hadn't asked him anything.

Jacob felt suddenly nervous. This felt—intimate. And while that wouldn't usually bother him, in fact he'd quite enjoy it normally, with the princess it was entirely too tempting. Too dangerous.

She still didn't speak, just stared at him with those wide chocolate-coloured eyes.

Using Herculean strength, Jacob focused his mind on the task at hand.

He lifted a not altogether steady hand to her face and brushed a curl back from where the blood had dried at her temple.

Her slight wince reminded him that she was hurt and scared, and that served to keep his mind on the task and not on the satiny smoothness of her skin.

Jacob worked diligently and soundlessly, dipping a linen into the hot water and gently wiping at the cut.

To his intense relief, it was more a scrape than anything else, and it wasn't deep enough to cause concern. Though there was a goodly sized bump to show for her efforts.

When he was done, Jacob risked eye contact.

Once again, the impact of her wide, innocent gaze was like a punch to the gut.

He cleared his throat again.

"I think you'll live." He smiled, ignoring the rough quality to his voice. "But no more boxing matches with trees."

She laughed softly, her breath fanning against his cheek, and desire slammed into him like a bolt of lightning.

Jacob jumped to his feet and busied himself with cleaning up the mess of used linens and disposing of the water.

When he felt as though he could breathe without wanting to devour the princess, he returned and took his seat across from her.

"Are you hungry?" he asked wryly, as he took in her look of longing as she stared at the spread before her.

"Famished." She grinned.

"You don't mind sharing?" he asked as he pushed a cup of tea toward her.

She sipped at the liquid before releasing a sigh of contentment.

"This is wonderful," she said effusively. "And no, I don't mind sharing. It seems the least I can do."

Jacob felt strangely content that they'd reached a sort of comfortable understanding.

They ate in companionable silence for a moment or two, and he was relieved to see some of the pallor leave her face.

"Feeling better?" he asked when she sat back.

"Much. I didn't realise how hungry I was. Or how tired."

She flicked a strand of hair over her shoulder and Jacob found himself staring at it, mesmerized by the way it bounced back into place.

"W-well, you've had a trying day," he answered gruffly. "A good night's sleep will see you to rights."

His words seemed to freeze the very air around the princess, and her eyes snapped up to his, huge and untrusting.

Jacob couldn't blame her. *Didn't* blame her. But he also didn't relish the idea of sleeping under the stars.

He would. He had, in fact, many times.

But it wouldn't be his first choice of venue.

"I'll just tend to the fire then leave you to sleep," he said to put her mind at ease.

"Are you leaving?" she blurted suddenly, blushing scarlet under his stare.

Jacob wondered at the question and her reaction to it.

"I'm going to stay outside. Just for tonight," he assured her hurriedly. "Once I check your head in the morning, I will leave you in peace."

She didn't need to know that he'd be close by. He could keep her safe and remain undetected for as long as necessary.

"Oh." She was still blushing, and her nerves seemed

to have returned in spades, if the hand wringing was anything to go by. Jacob wished he knew what she was thinking.

But he was rather enjoying the ceasefire and had no wish to anger her again.

He went over and added some more hastily gathered sticks and twigs to the fire. Tomorrow, he'd make sure to get her some proper firewood.

Turning back to face her, Jacob felt more awkward than he should.

He was one of Aldonia's best, most sophisticated agents.

Why then was he acting like a green lad at a brothel?

"If you need me, I'll be right outside," he said softly into the ever-growing tension.

"T-thank you," she mumbled, dropping her gaze to his rumpled cravat.

"Well, goodnight then, Miss Royal."

He waited but she didn't respond, so he turned and walked to the door.

Just as he turned the handle, however, she called out.

"Mr. Lauer?"

Jacob turned his head back, his heart twisting as he took in the sight of her standing in the firelight.

She didn't speak further, so he raised a brow and waited.

"You—" Her tongue darted out to wet her lips, and Jacob's gut clenched in reaction.

He had to get the hell out of there. Fast.

"You will be just outside?"

And then Jacob realised.

She *wanted* him here.

Rationally, he knew it was likely because she'd never been completely alone before. And because the forest in the dark was a frightening place. Especially when one only had a rickety old cottage for shelter.

Yet, this awareness still didn't stop the burst of pleasure he felt at knowing she wanted him around.

"Just outside," he confirmed softly.

Her smile had him clenching his fists against emotions he had no business feeling.

Jacob sketched a quick bow then moved swiftly outside before he did something irredeemably foolish.

But he couldn't keep the smile from his face.

Chapter Thirteen

"GOOD MORNING."

Harriet screeched in fright as the door swung open with a bang and sunlight poured into the darkened room.

She leapt from the bed then immediately regretted it when her head began to swim.

Sitting back down with a thump, she managed to scowl in Mr. Lauer's direction.

All night she'd been unable to sleep, thinking about him being outside.

Though she was loath to admit it, even to herself, the knowledge that he was out there watching over her had made Harriet feel safe and secure.

She knew that with those broad shoulders and that aura of power, he would be able to take care of anyone and anything he set his mind to.

But along with the safety came the uncertainty.

The feelings he evoked in her—aside from anger,

irritation, and exasperation—were confusing. New and dangerous and most inconvenient.

That was why she'd tossed and turned on the surprisingly comfortable cot. Why she'd been unable to sleep until the sounds outside the cottage told her dawn was breaking.

Even when she'd slept, she'd dreamt of a golden-haired Adonis with a charming grin and an interfering nature.

And now here he was, bursting into her solitude and looking far better than anyone had a right to at this hour of the morning.

"I didn't wake you, did I?" he asked, all joviality.

She felt like scratching his eyes out.

"Yes, you did, as it happens."

Her tart response only seemed to amuse him, and that dimpled grin that had sent her brain scrambling the day before made an appearance.

"You're not a morning person, Miss Royal?" he quipped.

Harriet chose to ignore him.

She stood up carefully, waiting to make sure the room didn't tilt.

Mr. Lauer seemed to notice her hesitance and immediately, all traces of joking were gone. His bright blue eyes darkened with concern, as did his expression.

"Are you well, Miss Royal? Is it your head?"

"I'm quite well," she responded, trying and failing

to stifle a yawn. "I just didn't sleep very well and wasn't expecting to be woken so *loudly.*"

The grin reappeared.

"My, my. Aren't we grumpy in the morning?"

Harriet barely supressed a growl.

How could she have been dreaming of those eyes as they'd sparkled down at her? Those hands as he'd caressed her face while tending to her cut?

He was the most exasperating person she'd ever met.

"Did you want something?" she asked piously, refusing to be goaded into losing her temper.

To Harriet's surprise, his eyes darkened even further until the blue was almost black, and she felt the inexplicable urge to fan herself.

Within seconds however, the affable rogue was back, and Harriet was left feeling vaguely unsettled.

"I think a cup of tea and some breakfast will cheer you right up," he said pleasantly, as he picked up the water bucket and began to make his way back outside. "Do relax, Miss Royal. I'll have you fed and watered in no time."

Either ignoring or not hearing her gasp of outrage, he swept outside, leaving her to stare after him.

All of last night's softening toward him went out the window.

His high-handedness was as bad as ever and once more, Harriet was left feeling as though her adventure were being taken over by the arrogant cad.

She stood from the bed and stomped over to the fireplace. She might as well make herself useful, since her life was being decided for her yet again.

Harriet was cleaning out the grate, being careful with the still-smoking embers, when the door opened once more and was filled with the figure of Mr. Lauer. He made the already small space seem tiny, filling every part of it with his presence.

"What are you doing?"

Harriet ignored the question, tried to ignore the presence of the domineering man.

A fete nigh on impossible to achieve, since he'd just come and crouched beside her.

"Here, let me do that," he said as he reached out to take the small shovel from her hand.

Harriet gritted her teeth as he gently jostled her out of the way.

"Why don't you find something to eat. Or fill the kettle?"

He smiled at her as though he were a kindly governess, and Harriet's temper flared.

This was the exact sort of thing she'd run away from.

She stood up and marched over to the valise filled with her clothing, snatching up a clean muslin and fresh undergarments.

She rooted around in the bottom of the bag before

pulling a bar of lavender-scented soap from its cloth. Next she snatched up her comb, tooth powder, and boar-hair toothbrush.

Finally, she shoved her feet into the kid boots she'd dropped by the bed and marched toward the door, her arms filled with her belongings.

"What are you doing?"

Mr. Lauer's surprised question stopped Harriet in her tracks, and she turned to glare at him.

"Since I seem to have lost the run of my cottage to an interloper, I thought I would go and bathe in the lake. I trust that you don't expect to *help* me with that?"

Once again, his eyes darkened at her question and raked her from head to toe. Harriet's heart stuttered then slammed against her chest, her entire body heating under that molten scrutiny.

"Of course not." His tone was husky and deep, and Harriet felt as though it burrowed under her skin to run along her veins like potent brandy.

"Well, good," she managed to huff, but her voice was high and breathless, even to her own ears.

There was a painfully tense moment where they stared at each other.

Harriet had no idea what Mr. Lauer was thinking, but he probably wasn't wondering what it would be like to kiss her.

Not that *she* was thinking that about *him,* of course.

Feeling her cheeks heat once again, Harriet turned

tail and fled from the cottage, putting some much-needed distance between Mr. Lauer and her treacherous body.

JACOB STARTED A fire, collected fresh water from a stream that ran down from the nearby mountain and put it on to heat before he even contemplated going to check on Princess Harriet.

He knew she was going to wash and change her clothing, and there was no way in hell he'd survive coming upon her in the middle of any of that.

She was angry. For a change, he thought sarcastically.

Jacob wracked his brain thinking what he could have done to upset her this time, but he was stumped.

Perhaps she was just highly strung all the time.

Though she did say she hadn't slept.

Well, the water she used to wash herself with would certainly cool her temper. Jacob had felt its iciness only an hour ago when he'd bathed himself.

He set out the last of her bread, cheese, and cured meat on the table.

One meal left. That was it. And plenty of tea.

No more linens. No medical supplies.

The reminder of her injury sent him out of the cottage and in search of the contrary royal before she hurt herself further.

He'd only walked a few minutes, following the fresh prints lest she had gotten it into her head to run off again, away from the lake. But before long, he arrived at the small lake he'd washed in earlier.

He steeled himself for what he might find. If she was naked, he'd simply have to avert his eyes and be a professional.

Jacob placed his hands on his hips and lifted his face to the sky, breathing deep and preparing for whatever he might find in front of him.

"What are you doing?"

Jacob screeched and nearly jumped out of his skin as the voice sounded right beside him.

He turned to glare down at the princess, unimpressed with her giggling.

"I'm sorry," she gasped. "I didn't mean to frighten you. That scream could wake the dead."

Jacob scowled his displeasure.

"Excuse me, madam," he bit out. "I did not scream."

"Oh no?" she laughed. "What would you call it then?"

Jacob eyed her, singularly unimpressed. She had scared the damned wits out of him. And he had *not* screamed.

"I yelled," he sniffed. "In a manly fashion."

For some reason, that just made her laugh harder.

Jacob wasn't used to feeling embarrassed, and it wasn't an emotion he enjoyed.

But as he eyed the freshly scrubbed princess with her rosy cheeks and that glorious hair only half-tied with a ribbon making her look innocently lovely, he felt his own lips twitch in response to her laughter.

At least she didn't appear to be angry at him anymore.

"I've left a pot of water on the fire, you know." He tried to bring things back to some sort of sensibility, but his words set her off into peals of laughter again.

"How is that funny?" he demanded.

"You sound just like one of our cooks, Mrs. Bremmer," she giggled. "Scolding me about the water and screeching like you've found a mouse in your kitchen."

Jacob had long since had a reputation of almost mythical success when it came to ladies. Hans had often complained that one flash of his dimples had even the most sophisticated woman swooning like a schoolgirl.

Never had he been compared to a screeching cook with a rodent problem.

And he didn't much care for it.

Desperate to ease some of his humiliation, Jacob tried to assert some authority.

"Let's get you back to the cottage so I can look at your head. Then once you've eaten, we will need to think about our next steps because you are out of supplies already."

He watched her expression go from amused to bemused, to downright furious. The sparkle of humour in her eyes changed to a glint of anger.

And once more, those tell-tale hands planted themselves on her hips, which was quite the fete considering one of them held her belongings all bundled up in yesterday's dress.

"I beg your pardon?"

Damn. He was in trouble again.

He'd never clashed so frequently with another person in his life. Not even enemies he'd interrogated, or captors who'd interrogated him.

"What?" he asked defensively. Perhaps even a little petulantly, he acknowledged. But only to himself.

"I don't need you checking my head or deciding when I should eat. Or what I should eat. Or *how* I should eat."

Her voice grew shriller with every word, but he felt it best not to flinch at the tone.

"And what will you do?" he asked, his own temper sparking to life. Never had he met a more infuriating female in his life. "Starve to death?"

"Of course not," she bit out before she suddenly took off, marching back toward the cottage.

"Then what?" he demanded, easily keeping pace with her shorter strides. "Because out here, you need my help and you're getting it whether you want it or not."

They reached the cottage and Princess Harriet threw her bundle haphazardly on the bed before spinning to glower at him.

"You can't help me against my will. I forbid it," she yelled.

Jacob raised a brow. She needed to be more careful. Her princess was showing.

"You forbid it?" he questioned and watched as her eyes widened. "Do you make a habit of ordering people around as though you had a right to, Miss *Royal*?"

As he'd expected, she began to blush furiously at his goading.

"No, of course not." She tripped over the words, more flustered than he'd seen her thus far. "I just – I don't appreciate your interference. But I know I can't order people about. How silly."

Her laugh was as brittle as the fake smile she had plastered on her face.

The water on the fire began to spill over, so Jacob rushed to remove it. Wordlessly, Harriet began to prepare tea. They worked together in silence for a moment or two then by unspoken consent, they both sat at the table.

It was unusually intimate and domesticated, and Jacob wasn't entirely happy about that.

Clearing his throat, he determined to re-erect the border between the princess being a job, and being someone who was far too attractive for his peace of mind.

"So, Miss Royal." He watched as she poured tea, every inch the Society lady. She should have looked out of place in such modest surroundings. Even without a crown she was the epitome of regal. Yet she seemed just as comfortable in a rundown cabin on a rickety chair as she was sure to be in a gilded hall on a golden throne. "How do you manage to survive out here then, if you refuse to let me help you, and you insist on staying hidden?"

She blinked at him, her wide, chocolate eyes doing their best to affect him. But he was strong. He was a spy, for God's sake. He could withstand a pair of eyes.

She was quiet for a moment, nibbling distractedly on her bottom lip before she tilted her chin.

"I'll live off the land," she sniffed, and Jacob had to work to keep a straight face.

He knew she'd be spitting mad if he allowed his grin to break free.

"Live off the land," he repeated. "How?"

"Well, you know," she stuttered. "I'll fish and—and hunt, and—" She cleared her throat nervously, looking less sure of herself with every passing second. "Forage for berries and such."

Jacob quirked a brow, earning one of her scowls.

"I don't know why I was worried," he drawled sarcastically. "Clearly, you're an expert in all things survival."

That earned him an eye roll and a long-suffering sigh.

"And I suppose you are?" she snapped.

"I am, as it happens," he answered. "And I know with absolute certainty that if you go "foraging for berries" you don't recognise, you'll be dead within two days."

Her cheeks paled and he felt a momentary guilt at having been so harsh. But she needed to know there were limits to what she could do.

And it would make Jacob's job a hell of a lot easier if the princess actually *wanted* him around.

He thought back to last night, when he suspected she'd wanted him there.

Perhaps if reason wouldn't work, her own fears might.

"I'll go if you want me to, of course." He kept his tone even as he cut a piece of cheese from his own modest portion. "I just hope nobody else finds you out here."

Chapter Fourteen

*H*ARRIET STUDIED MR. Lauer's face to see if he was trying to trick her or scare her. But his expression was open and polite. No mischief in his blue eyes that she could see.

He might not have meant to scare her with his words, but he had done so.

She was very aware of the threat to her family and now that she'd run away, she had no way of knowing if Christopher had taken care of it. She was inclined to think he *had* because that was Christopher, capable and efficient in all things.

But what if he hadn't handled it? What if there was an army of assassins out there trying to kill her entire family? Trying to kill her?

With dawning horror and panic, Harriet faced up to the reality of her situation.

If someone came looking for her, she was out here exposed. All because she wasn't willing to spend time with Althea Furberg.

Worse, she had isolated herself so that she wouldn't be privy to any information about Christopher, or her parents, or anything else.

The bread that she'd been chewing on stuck in her throat, and she lifted her teacup with an unsteady hand.

"Miss Royal?"

Harriet looked up at the gentle voice. Mr. Lauer was studying her with something akin to concern stamped on his handsome face.

Their meeting had been unconventional to say the least. And he annoyed her more than any other living creature she'd ever met.

Yet he'd helped her when he didn't have to.

Had slept outside and tended to her injury.

And, she was rather selfishly just realising, he hadn't even completed his own journey since he'd stayed with her.

"I've kept you from your plans," she blurted, worry for her family and shame at her self-interest making her voice wobbly. "I am sorry for that, Mr. Lauer."

He studied her intently, and Harriet wondered what he saw in her face.

His expression gentled and Harriet's heart fluttered.

"That's quite all right, Miss Royal," he said softly. "I had no fixed plans. And I'm rather enjoying my little adventure in the woods."

His grin was so incorrigible that Harriet found herself answering it with one of her own.

But her head was so filled with thoughts of her family that even his handsome face wasn't enough of a distraction.

"What is it, Miss Royal? I can tell something is bothering you."

"You know me so well," she joked with a small smile.

"I'm starting to," he answered softly and again, her heart flipped.

For a mad moment, Harriet was tempted to confess all to Mr. Lauer. To tell him who she really was. To give up on the whole thing and go home.

She'd feel like a failure for the rest of her life but the alterative was to stay out here, isolated and unaware of everything.

But she couldn't tell him.

As soon as he found out who she was, he would change. Everyone did.

And while she couldn't imagine him being syco-phantic, he was a man of integrity, she knew. And he wouldn't allow her to stay here undiscovered. Not when she was sure that Christopher had sent guards looking for her.

"I suppose I'm just worried about – about sup-plies," she lied. "I can't exactly forage for bread, for example."

Mr. Lauer studied her with that intense look again before his expression cleared and he was all cheerfulness again.

"No, you can't. If you don't mind my staying around a little longer, perhaps I could go to the village and pick up some supplies?"

Harriet tried to hide her relief.

"Thank you, Mr. Lauer, I would appreciate that."

"It is my pleasure, Miss Royal. Besides, I quite like to catch up on village gossip while I'm here."

"You do? Well then, I suppose you'll get all the news from the locals."

She fought to keep her voice steady but she couldn't believe her luck. If anything was going on with the royal family it wold make its way here, Harriet was sure of it.

Gossip, after all, travelled fast.

And he'd find out if there were any guards searching for her, too.

Harriet hopped to her feet and rushed over to get her bag of coin.

She reeled off a shopping list from the top of her head, not really caring what he brought back as long as he brought news with it.

Within minutes, she was rushing her unexpected companion to the door.

Before he left however, he swung around to face

her, and his face was as serious as she'd ever seen it.

"Do not venture too far," he warned. "And don't let anyone in. Anyone at all."

She blinked up at him in surprise. If she didn't know any better, she'd think that he knew about the threat to her family.

"I won't," she promised.

His gaze was intent upon her face for a moment before he nodded.

"I'll be as quick as I can," he said. "Though the journey will take some time. Stay safe and rest if you can. No more bumps to the head."

He reached out and touched a gentle hand to the side of her head where the bump from yesterday still remained, and Harriet's heart stopped dead in her chest at the contact.

All of a sudden the very air in the room seemed charged, and Harriet found herself moving closer to him.

The scent of sandalwood soap surrounded him, and a potent desire unfurled in her belly.

His eyes dropped to hers, his cobalt gaze trapping her.

Harriet couldn't have moved if God Himself commanded it. How could one innocent touch evoke such a response in her?

Her breath stuttered and her stomach flipped and all she could do was stand there, hopelessly gazing into his face.

Without conscious thought, Harriet stepped closer until she could feel the heat from his body.

Her heart thumped so loudly she could practically hear it echoing around the room.

He was staring at her as though he could see into her very soul.

Time seemed to stand still.

"Jacob."

She didn't know what she wanted to say. She hadn't even consciously said his name.

But her voice, like the rest of her, seemed to be out of her control. The throaty whisper sounding his name like a plea.

And then, with a muffled oath, he reached out and pulled her into his arms, before bending and capturing her mouth in a kiss that set her whole world on fire.

THE SECOND JACOB'S lips touched Princess Harriet's, every modicum of sense left his body and he was moved by feeling and instinct alone.

It didn't matter that she was an assignment. It didn't matter that she was the Crown Princess. It didn't matter that she didn't even know who he really was.

His entire mind, his whole body, was consumed with her—the taste of her lips, the feel of her body pressed torturously against his own.

He couldn't stifle an agonised groan as she reached up to clasp his neck, pulling herself impossibly close to him, stoking the inferno inside him to an unbearable heat.

Lowering his hands, he pressed her closer still, and her gasp allowed him to deepen their kiss, to explore her mouth in a way that was both exquisite and excruciating.

The kiss went on and on, and Jacob could no more have stopped it than stopped the sun from rising.

He didn't want to stop it.

Over the years he'd had more than his share of encounters with women. Women with experience. Sophistication. Knowledge of the opposite sex.

And none of them had made him feel a fraction of what he was feeling now, with Princess Harriet's innocent kiss.

Jacob was just about to drag his unruly body back under his control when he felt the hesitant touch of Harriet's tongue as she mimicked his actions.

Well, hell, he thought. *A man can only withstand so much.*

With a muffled, desperate oath against her lips, he turned them so she was pressed against the wall of the cottage.

He moved his hands to capture her face, angled her head, and once more delved his tongue inside her incredibly sweet mouth.

His body trapped hers completely against the wall, but she didn't seem to mind.

In fact, her desperate little moans were driving him beyond reason, beyond any hope of control.

May the devil take him for the blackguard he was, for he wanted nothing more than to lift her skirts and finish what he'd been foolish enough to start.

That wild, animalistic thought was enough to stop Jacob in his tracks and allow him to claw back a tiny bit of sense.

What the hell was he doing? She was an innocent. A princess, damn it.

And here he was, ready to take her against a bloody wall.

Jacob ripped his mouth from hers and with a strength he didn't think he possessed, took a deliberate step back from her and the tempting scent of lavender that surrounded her.

He bowed his head, hearing her haggard breathing that matched his own.

When he felt as though he could look at her again without ravishing her on the spot, Jacob looked up.

And very nearly dragged her into his arms again.

The ribbon in her hair had come undone so it fell around her shoulders in a waterfall of sable curls.

Her eyes were huge and dark, gazing at him with wonder and desire.

Inside him, the beast awakened by his lust roared to life at the look in her eyes, but already the stark reality of what he'd done was racing through his mind.

Jacob knew he needed to apologise. Knew he needed to assure her that he would never touch her again.

Yet it was harder to do than it should have been because truthfully, he wasn't sorry at all.

How could he be when the taste of her had been like nothing he'd ever experienced?

Brutally pushing aside the exquisite memory of having her in his arms, Jacob dragged in some much-needed air.

In all his years of working for Prince Christopher, he'd never lost control. Not once. Not for any reason.

Three days with the princess, and he was ready to throw his whole life away just to hold her in his arms once more.

He kept his eyes on her, on the laboured breathing, on the furious blush that now stained her cheeks.

God, she was beautiful; it almost hurt to look at her.

And now that he knew what it was to kiss her…

"I'm sorry, Miss Royal. My actions were unpardonable. I can assure you, that won't happen again."

Would she believe him? Would she feel unsafe with him now? Had he just blown this whole assignment and consequentially, his entire career?

Princess Harriet didn't speak, or even move, for an

eternity.

Finally, she meekly nodded then lowered her head to gaze furiously at the floor.

Jacob could only hope that she wouldn't run the second he left the cottage.

He was tempted to stay just to make sure, but he wanted to give her some distance, and he sure as hell wanted to give himself some.

Besides, he'd yet to write to Prince Christopher to brief him on the situation.

A sudden, uncomfortable guilt began to slither along Jacob's veins, as though he didn't have enough emotions to contend with.

Here she thought she'd just been kissed senseless by a helpful stranger.

Lying to her was starting to feel like a betrayal. Yet what choice did he have?

Heaving a sigh, Jacob decided to risk going into the village.

If she did run, it would be child's play to track her down.

"I'll be back soon, Miss Royal," he said for want of anything else to say.

Still, she hadn't spoken, and Jacob felt sick that he might have scared her.

He moved swiftly to the door, determined to put as much space between him and the tempting princess as possible.

"Wait."

Right before he left, she called out, stopping him dead.

Jacob turned to face her, fascinated by the deepening of her blush.

She heaved a deep breath then looked him squarely in the eyes.

"I think you should call me Harriet," she said, a small smile playing around her mouth. "And *do* come back soon."

Chapter Fifteen

━━━━❦━━━━

*I*T HAD BEEN hours, yet Harriet still couldn't concentrate on anything but the memory of that explosive kiss.

Not only had she been thoroughly kissed for the first time, but she'd also made sure that the man who'd kissed her came back for round two!

Harriet could feel her cheeks heat with the memory of her boldness.

When Mr. Lauer—Jacob, really, since propriety had long since become redundant—had been apologising, she'd been afraid that he'd genuinely regretted kissing her. That somehow she'd done it wrong or it had been unpleasant for him.

And yet, a scorching flame of desire had still danced in his eyes, even as he'd been speaking.

In fact, for one, mad moment, Harriet had thought he meant to do it again. And she had wanted him to, quite desperately.

She wondered what the people of Aldonia would make of their princess, alone in the woods with a handsome stranger, calling him by his Christian name and kissing him with an ardour that bordered on desperation.

She remembered how desperate Alex had seemed at times around Lydia and how she had wondered at her brother's odd behaviour.

Now, she could understand it.

She thought of staid Christopher and the obsequious Lady Althea.

Could Christopher feel like that about the lady? Was that why he couldn't seem to see her for what she truly was?

Harriet had given up on trying to distract herself with one of the books she'd brought and had come outside to walk along the stream.

But nothing could stop her thoughts from repeatedly circling back to Jacob.

She should be embarrassed by her conduct. Ashamed and disgraced.

But she quite simply couldn't bring herself to regret their embrace.

And she'd known from the look on his face that he'd been worried she'd run away.

But she wouldn't.

It was the oddest thing, she mused as she watched a lone bird wheel through the clear, blue sky.

He had angered her, infuriated her, goaded her more than anyone she'd ever met.

Yet now that he was gone and she was alone just as she'd planned, she *missed* him.

And now that she knew what it was to be kissed by him…

Harriet's heart fluttered alarmingly.

If it wasn't too soon, if she didn't know better, she'd think herself to be falling in love with the irascible man.

But surely not.

It would be futile in any case.

Her father would never allow her to marry an untitled man of little consequence. Even if he was the most handsome one she'd ever seen. Even if he did make her heart beat rapidly and her stomach riot with butterflies.

She thought of Aunt Anya and her move to England to be with the man she loved.

Thought of Alex and Lydia, also in England and living in bucolic bliss.

If they could do it—

But, no. It was folly indeed to be thinking such things.

Jacob was a man of the world, Harriet was sure. It was entirely possible that the kiss had meant nothing to him.

And if her stomach clenched painfully at that

thought well then, she'd just have to deal with it.

Sophisticated ladies of the world, she was quite sure, didn't lose the run of themselves over one kiss.

Jacob would return soon, hopefully not with news about her family. No news would mean they were safe.

And this little escapade couldn't last forever.

Just two weeks, she decided. Just long enough to prove to Christopher that she could take charge of her own life. Make her own decisions.

Long enough for the awful Furbergs to return home without her.

And long enough, she hoped scandalously, to enjoy more wicked assignations with her Mr. Lauer.

JACOB TRACKED HARRIET'S steps toward the stream.

She hadn't run away. Not with all of her things strewn about the cottage.

She wasn't very tidy, he observed with a grin. He had no idea why he found that endearing.

Perhaps it was just that the perfect little princess had a flaw.

When his heart sped in anticipation of seeing her, he knew he was in more trouble than he'd reckoned.

And the guilt he felt at misleading her was growing stronger with every step he took.

He'd written to Prince Christopher. Assured the

man that his sister was well and in Jacob's care.

He'd thought it prudent to leave out the part where he'd devoured the princess like a starving man at a feast.

He'd also apprised the prince of their location, assuring him that he'd keep her here for at least another week before returning home.

At least now the prince knew where to write to Jacob. If he was needed back at the palace, or indeed if the would-be assassin was apprehended, Jacob would know to bring the princess back.

His gut clenched at the idea of their woodland interlude ending. Which was utter madness, of course.

They couldn't stay there forever. He didn't *want* to stay there forever, he assured himself. But even in his head, the words sounded hollow.

And Jacob refused to even contemplate examining why that was. It was far too terrifying.

He shouldn't have to work this hard to remember his duty. He shouldn't have to warn himself over and over again that touching her had been folly. Dangerous, even. Something that absolutely shouldn't and couldn't be repeated.

Just as Jacob reached a small clearing, the princess came into view, and his whole body jerked with a heady mixture of desire and something tender and altogether frightening.

He didn't make a sound. Didn't alert her to his

presence.

He just stood and looked his fill.

She was beautiful enough to make a man weep.

He was pleased to see that she hadn't retied her hair. It still fell loose around her shoulders and down her back, making his hands itch to run through the silky strands.

She was standing by the water, gazing into its babbling depths, and he found himself wanting to know, quite desperately, what she was thinking.

Jacob was in more trouble than he'd ever been in his life.

He stepped forward, a twig snapping beneath his boot.

Knowing that he couldn't touch her again was a torture the likes of which he'd never before experienced.

Princess Harriet swung around at the sound of his approach, and the smile that lit her face damn near took his breath away.

It was going to be harder than he'd thought keeping his hands off her.

But he was a professional. He was good at what he did. Excellent, in fact. Nothing had ever broken him before. Nothing.

The princess hurried over to him.

Jacob gritted his teeth, reminded himself how impossible she was. How the sweet, innocent exterior hid a stubborn viper with a cutting tongue.

Don't bloody think of her tongue, he told himself fiercely.

The princess came to a stop in front of him. Close enough for him to see the flecks of gold in her chocolate-brown eyes.

Close enough for him to smell the lavender that clung to her skin.

Nothing had broken him before. Nothing.

He said the words like a litany in his head.

"You're back," she said a little breathlessly.

There was a look in her eyes that he couldn't name. Determination, perhaps.

"I am," he croaked.

Nothing had broken him before.

Before he could speak again, the princess shocked him to his core by grabbing hold of his superfine, reaching up, and pressing her lips against his own.

He stood stock still for a millisecond before once again his desire for the lady took over mind, body, and soul.

He was broken.

This tiny woman with her huge brown eyes and smart mouth had broken him.

Chapter Sixteen

‹◦›

THE DAYS MARCHED on and Harriet and Jacob created a whole life for themselves in the tiny corner of the woods, a life removed from reality.

It had been almost two weeks of bliss.

Even though their moments of pleasure were interspersed with the arguments that seemed to crop up at the slightest provocation, there was never any real anger in their interactions.

He couldn't help it if she had no stomach for catching and preparing a rabbit, or quail for example.

Nor could he help it that she had no talent for fishing, despite hours of tutelage.

He found himself *enjoying* that temper of hers. Just as he'd found himself enjoying the novels she'd brought with her, though he made sure to hide his reading from her, knowing she'd tease him mercilessly about his avid interest in such nonsensical, romantic tosh.

Perhaps strangest of all, however, Jacob had found himself opening up to Harriet. Telling her about the turbulent relationship he'd always had with his father, who seemed constantly disappointed in him. And about his Nordic mother from whom he'd gotten his fair colouring and who had died before he'd ever truly known her.

And he spoke of his travels, though he was always careful not to give too much away. Even when he wanted to spill his heart out, and tell her everything, he knew that he could not.

Jacob felt as though he'd become two completely separate men.

There was the agent who travelled into the village every day to check for messages from the prince. The one who ran a gauntlet of negative emotions from guilt to fear to apprehension. The man who thought about when all this was over and what it would mean for him and for Harriet.

And then there was the man who spent every day falling deeper under Harriet's spell. The man whose heart felt lighter, whose life felt more meaningful, just by being close to her.

That man, he knew, was dangerously close to throwing away everything he'd ever worked for, just to stay by her side.

That man, he feared, had fallen irrevocably in love.

But although he enjoyed the routine they'd fallen

into, although he couldn't remember a happier time in his life, every day his uneasiness grew.

He tried to tell himself that Princess Harriet had lied to him, too. Was hiding who she really was, just as Jacob was doing.

But it wasn't the same thing, and he knew it.

Harriet was lying because she wanted an experience free from the strictures of her title.

Her lies weren't hurting anyone.

His, he knew, would hurt Harriet. The one person he'd rather die than hurt.

Yet, it was painfully inevitable.

The truth would come out.

And he would lose her forever.

"Jacob, are you listening to me?"

Jacob dragged himself from his depressing thoughts to see Harriet, hands planted firmly on her hips, glaring at him.

Just a week ago, that look would have irritated him. Or worried him.

Now, he knew that he could coax her from any bad mood with a kiss, even a particular look.

And it was no hardship.

In fact, some days he annoyed her on purpose just so he could cheer her up again.

The only saving grace for his conduct was the fact that he never allowed things to go further than kisses, albeit explosive, earth-shattering ones.

It wasn't much, but it was enough to help his conscious a little.

Much as he desperately wanted to, much as his body raged against him, he never allowed himself to go down a path there was no coming back from.

And though he could sense Harriet's frustration, a frustration that tried his gentlemanliness more than he could put into words, he managed to hang on to that one, last boundary between them.

But as time went on, as day after day was spent talking for hours while he attempted to teach her to fish, and showed her which berries were likely to kill her, and where to hunt out quail eggs, and nights were spent with her wrapped in his arms, testing his resolve and ensuring that he never got a decent sleep, kept awake by his desperate, almost savage desire for her, Jacob's resolve was growing weaker.

Soon, he knew, the thread would snap. Soon, her desperate throaty pleas would bring the cage around his desire tumbling down. And Jacob would never forgive himself.

Princess Harriet had no idea what she was begging him for in the small, dark hours of the night. She was a temptress beyond even her own comprehension.

And it was the knowledge of her innocence, and his subterfuge, that kept him steadfast in his determination to keep her innocent.

But he could only withstand so much. He was, after

all, just a man. And a flawed one at that.

"Jacob!"

Her exasperated tone warned him that his mind had wandered again.

"Sorry, love." He grinned, hoping to charm her.

Judging by the pink blush that stained her cheeks, it was working.

She still rolled her eyes though.

"I asked you to pass me that bowl."

They'd gone berry picking just that morning, and Harriet was diligently washing the plump fruit.

That was another thing Jacob couldn't help but admire about the princess.

His assumption that she'd be spoilt, pampered, and demanding had been wrong.

While there was no denying that she couldn't do a lot because she'd never had to, she was willing and eager to learn all manner of things. She had a quick mind, and she was never afraid of hard work.

He'd taught her how to cook. He'd taught her how to hunt out eggs and at least try to catch fish. And while she shied away from some of the more gruesome tasks involved in preparing their food, she didn't mind getting her hands dirty doing everything else.

Grabbing the bowl, Jacob moved to place it on the table beside where she stood. He grabbed her round the waist, pulling her back to lean against his chest, delighting in her breathless giggles as he placed a series of kisses along her neck.

"Don't you have anything to do?" she tried to scold him, even as she leaned back to give him better access.

"What could be better than this?" he growled against her throat.

To his surprise, she stiffened at his words.

Jacob let her go and stepped back, allowing her to turn to face him.

She was working up to something. He recognized the signs.

A deep breath followed by a determined tilt of her chin.

"I can think of something better," she said, boldly meeting his gaze.

Jacob froze at her words.

He wasn't stupid. He knew what she meant.

And even if he hadn't, her scalded cheeks were something of a giveaway.

"Harriet." He kept his tone even but instilled it with a warning.

It was bad enough fighting himself. He couldn't fight her, too.

He didn't have the strength.

"You don't know what you're saying," he bit out.

She watched him in silence for a moment, and Jacob resisted the urge to turn away from her.

He didn't want her seeing the truth in his eyes, the lust that he kept at bay by sheer force of will only.

"I do know what I'm saying."

The steadiness in her voice surprised him. But then, it shouldn't have.

Harriet had a strength inside her that he'd rarely seen before.

"No, you don't."

Now he did turn away, busied himself at a fire that didn't need stoking.

"Yes, I do."

He heard the steel in her tone that said her temper was rising.

"We're not discussing this," he bit out.

"Oh, yes, we are."

Jacob closed his eyes and prayed for patience. When that didn't work, he prayed again. Harder.

"Harriet." He turned to face her then.

This wasn't a conversation he thought they'd have, and he hadn't a damn clue what to say.

"Why are you doing this now?" He tried to sound placating. Instead, he sounded pleading.

"Because we—that is you—" She stumbled to a halt and dropped her eyes to the floor. "I thought you wanted—"

Jacob frowned at her in confusion until realisation dawned and a bark of shocked laughter escaped.

"You think I don't *want* you?" He laughed but it sounded strangled, even to his own ears.

"It's not funny," she said through gritted teeth.

"No, it's not," he glowered.

Taking a steadying breath, he moved over to clasp her hands in his own larger ones.

Whatever the temptation of being so close during a conversation like *this,* he wouldn't have her thinking that she wasn't the most desirable woman on the earth.

"Harriet." He trapped her gaze with his own, not allowing her to look away. "I want you so much that it kills me," he said bluntly. "I haven't slept in two bloody weeks. Being this close to you and not doing what I so desperately crave is torture."

Her eyes widened at his words, and he marvelled at it.

How could she doubt her own desirability?

"Then why—"

"I care about you too much to ruin you, Harriet."

Harriet swallowed hard.

"I care about you, too," she confessed, and he knew a moment of pure, unadulterated elation. "Enough to not want this to end."

God, he couldn't let her start talking about a future he knew wasn't possible.

"Jacob." She blinked up at him. "I think, no I *know* that I lo—"

"Stop."

The word felt ripped from his soul. He couldn't be sure, of course, but he feared that she was about to tell him something he couldn't stand to hear. Not now.

Not when she had no idea that sooner or later, they were going to be ripped apart, even if it wasn't what they wanted.

He watched her flinch as though he'd slapped her, and his stomach twisted with regret, with fear, with anger at himself for allowing this to happen.

Harriet pulled her hands from his but she didn't move away.

"There are—" She hesitated before squaring her shoulders and ploughing on. "There are things about me that I haven't told you. About my family. About who I am. But, I won't let those things stop us from being together."

She stepped closer to him, and Jacob felt a desperate urge to back away from her.

"I didn't expect this to happen, but it has. And I'm glad of it. We can be together and—"

"Harriet," he cut off her words, each of them hurting like a knife.

He never should have started whatever this was between them. He had thought, foolishly perhaps, that they would be summoned back to Court, that he could spend that time explaining himself, begging for forgiveness.

But what explanation could possibly be good enough? How could he expect forgiveness?

Jacob steeled himself to say what needed to be said.

"What you want—what *I* want. It can't happen."

"It can," she insisted. He'd known she was tenacious, but it had never felt as though she were tearing out his heart before. "That's what I'm telling you. It can happen. It's what I want. I want to be with you. In *every* way."

Jacob gritted his teeth against the intense longing she evoked in him. It was tempting, so tempting to take what she was offering.

But he couldn't.

Not because of his job, or his loyalty to the prince. Not because he was lying, or because his guilt was clawing at him like a live thing.

But because he loved her too much to take such a precious gift when he wasn't who she would spend the rest of her life with.

There.

He'd admitted it. If only to himself.

He loved her. So much that he felt it in the very blood that flowed through his veins.

What an ungodly mess he'd made of his life.

"I'm going to the village," he blurted.

He needed to write to Prince Christopher. He needed to tell him that he was bringing the princess back, and then he was getting the hell out of Aldonia.

Harriet's jaw dropped.

"What?" she gasped, and he couldn't blame her.

It wasn't exactly an appropriate response to what she'd said.

"I'm sorry," he said sincerely, uselessly. "But I need to go."

He turned toward the door.

"Jacob?"

Her hurt and bewilderment was like a dagger to his heart.

"I don't understand. Why are you ignoring this? Why are you rejecting me?"

He couldn't bear to hear the hurt in her voice but couldn't stay here any longer, his resolve weakening with every second.

"I'm not," he managed. "I just need to go."

"Why?" she demanded.

Jacob swung back around to face her, every one of his roiling emotions crashing to the surface.

"Because I'm not going to ruin the Crown Princess of Aldonia," he yelled.

The silence swallowed his outburst, leaving only laboured breathing and shattered hearts in its wake.

Chapter Seventeen

*H*ARRIET HEARD JACOB'S words echoing around the room, ringing in her head.

But she couldn't make sense of them.

He knew. He *knew*?

But how? Nobody knew she was here. So, he couldn't have heard it at the village.

And that meant—oh God. That meant he'd always known.

Their chance meeting wasn't a chance meeting at all.

Everything that had happened for the past two weeks was a lie. Not real.

But the way she loved him. That was real. And the heartbreak she was feeling now. That was painfully, awfully, nightmarishly real.

"You know who I am."

It wasn't a question. It was a statement.

And it was in a voice she didn't recognise.

Inside, she felt as though her heart were splintering in two. Yet all those years of being groomed into the perfect princess had obviously paid off.

One didn't show emotion. And right now, nothing about Harriet showed her inner turmoil. Her voice was calm and cold. The voice of a stranger, even to her own ears.

Jacob looked stricken. Pained by his confession.

But Harriet couldn't even contemplate his feelings when she couldn't get a hold of her own.

"Yes," he said hoarsely.

She could only stare at him. For eons, she could only look into the face that she'd come to love so desperately, and wonder how he could have fooled her so. And *why*.

"I can explain," he continued, a tinge of desperation to his tone.

He reached out a hand, and she flinched away.

She was barely standing upright. If he touched her now, she'd break into a thousand pieces.

"Explain then," she bit out.

"Can we sit?"

She wanted to refuse, petulant though it was. But she felt as though her legs could give way any second and so wordlessly, she moved to one of the wooden chairs at the fire.

Her heart twisted as she thought of all the pleasant days she'd spent with him, sharing stories of childhood, sharing babbling conversations about everything and nothing, sharing silences filled with a comfort she'd come to hold so dear.

All of it was tainted now.

He sat across from her and gazed at her with cobalt eyes, his golden hair glinting in the firelight.

Usually, his handsomeness took her breath away. Now, it felt as though all her breath had been taken by his confession.

She didn't know what to do. And so, she listened.

And the longer he spoke, the more her heart broke.

Not just because she'd fallen in love with this man, this man who had only been with her because Christopher had commanded it.

But her wonderful adventure, her quest for independence and anonymity was a farce. Christopher had known.

And Harriet should have known; there was no such thing as freedom. Not for a royal.

She was humiliated. And heart sore. And suddenly, desperately tired.

She wanted to go home where she could lick her wounds in peace. She didn't even want to confront Christopher. She just wanted to lock herself away and cry.

Perhaps if Alex had come at Christopher's request, she would return to England with him after all. Some distance would do her the world of good right now.

Distance from Christopher and his unyielding management of her life.

Distance from Jacob.

Harriet swallowed a lump in her throat.

"So, you're some sort of secret agent, then? Working for my brother?"

It sounded impossible but then, when it came to Christopher and his iron control over his responsibilities, it didn't really surprise her.

"Yes."

She appreciated the simple reply. And the silence that followed it. She couldn't listen to apologies or platitudes now.

"How? How could this be? Does my father even know about you?"

To Harriet's amazement, Jacob shook his head.

"Prince Christopher is our only commander. We are his personal agents."

She was bewildered and even momentarily distracted from her tempestuous emotions.

"But, where did he find you?" she asked.

His smile was miniscule and fleeting.

"I was destined for the army. Started off there, in fact, As the second son of the Count of Dresbonne, my father had high hopes for me."

Harriet felt another jolt of shock. He was an aristocrat. Yet she never saw him at Court. She would have remembered.

"Unfortunately, I had a problem with authority, but my skills were such that they drew the prince's attention, and I've worked for him ever since."

A vague memory flashed briefly in her mind. A golden-haired boy soldier with a mischievous grin being dressed down by the captain.

"I saw you," she blurted. "As I child. I saw you in uniform. In the courtyard."

Jacob didn't say anything. What did it matter, in any case? She hadn't known him as a child. But she knew him now. And he knew her. More than anyone in her life.

Remembering the last two weeks, the things she'd told him about herself, the way he'd held her and kissed her—it made her sick with shame.

She'd even slept on the same bed as him. If he decided to tell tales about her, it would be all over the palace and then the rest of the city before she could blink.

And whereas thirty minutes ago she would have never thought him capable of doing something like that, Harriet realised that she didn't know this man. Not at all.

Because he wasn't who he said he was. And she wasn't important to him. She was a job. A chore he'd had to do for his prince.

She dropped her gaze to her tightly clasped hands not sure what to think, what to feel. Embarrassment waring with anger. Hate waring with desperate sadness.

"Harriet."

Just that one word, just her name, barely above a whisper, was enough for Harriet to know that she quite simply didn't have the strength to talk any more. Not about this. Not about anything.

If he touched her, if he tried to comfort her, or apologise, or feign any interest in her or how she was feeling, she'd lose all control. She'd sob, and scream, and humiliate herself even more.

Gathering what was left of her tattered dignity, and drawing on years of being brought up to be the absolute crème de la crème of a Society lady, Harriet drew her eyes up to look into his.

She refused to see despondency in their blue depths. Refused to think that was sorrow or concern or—her foolish heart stuttered—or tenderness.

"I want to go home."

He frowned slightly. Maybe at her tone. Maybe at the fact that she didn't comment on his detailed explanation. Harriet didn't much care.

And she didn't want to give him the chance to ask.

"I realise that you won't let me go alone, since my brother has presumably hired you to keep me safe and, if not well, at least alive."

His answering grimace was enough to tell her that she was at least partly right.

"I shall be ready to leave within the hour."

Harriet stood, pleased that she sounded and appeared poised when she felt anything but.

Wordlessly, she picked up her bags, placed them on the cot and began filling them.

Jacob stood, too, she noticed in her peripheral vision, and for the first time since Harriet had known him, he looked unsure, less than perfectly in control.

"Harriet. Sweetheart."

The pain in her heart at his endearment said in such a pleading tone nearly cleaved her heart in two.

She wouldn't survive a two-day journey back to the palace with him if she allowed him past her hastily constructed defences, even for a second.

Stiffening her shoulders and her resolve, Harriet turned to face him.

"I am the Crown Princess of Aldonia, Mr. Lauer," she said, her voice icy and emotionless. "You will address me as Your Highness, or Princess, or not at all."

Her words froze the air between them, and she could see that they'd hurt him. But it didn't affect her. She couldn't let it.

She was a princess, and he was an agent for her brother.

Harriet had known that this little adventure of hers couldn't last forever.

Foolishly, she'd begun to let herself imagine that it

could.

Not hidden away, of course. But she didn't need to hide away to have an adventure. Being with him forever would have been her greatest adventure. He would have been enough.

They stood and stared at each other for an age. Harriet refused to back down. Refused to break down. Refused to do anything other than give him her haughtiest look so he'd leave her alone.

"I'll prepare the horse," he finally said.

"You're dismissed then," she said coldly.

And she held onto her tears until he walked out and shut the door quietly behind him.

Chapter Eighteen

*S*HE HADN'T SPOKEN a word.

Not one single word.

A couple of weeks ago, Jacob would have been thrilled with that. Now, it just broke his damned heart.

True to her word, Harriet—or Princess Harriet—he thought with a pang, had been packed up within an hour.

She'd come outside the cottage and if the situation hadn't been so dire, he would have laughed at her carrying those damned bags again. Though she was able to manage them a lot better now, given they were practically empty, they still swamped either side of her.

It seemed a lifetime ago he'd watched her dragging them along the road from the village.

He'd been irritated by her tenacity then. Now, he loved it about her, just like he fiercely loved everything else about her.

He tried to take the bags, of course, but she'd ignored him, walking by with her chin in the air, regal as the princess that she was.

When she reached the tethered horse, she conceded to allowing his help, but instead of passing the bags to him like an adult, she dropped them on the ground.

Jacob gritted his teeth and didn't comment. He had no idea where things stood between them and he wasn't going to risk upsetting her further by commenting on her actions.

He'd hoped that she'd be full of questions; he wanted quite desperately for her to interrogate him. To rail against him. To scream. Hit him, even, if she wanted to.

But this quiet, subdued ice princess was killing him. It wasn't the Harriet he knew. The Harriet he loved.

She was a stranger.

They'd reached the hidden gig in silence. He'd hitched up the horse and packed up their luggage without a word.

She allowed him to help her into the conveyance because she hadn't had much choice, but she'd done it without uttering a sound, let alone a word.

And now, here they sat. Almost at the village, and she hadn't even moved her head in his direction.

"I'd like to see about procuring a private coach for your journey home, Harr—Your Highness," he said quietly. "I don't want you travelling on the mail coach, if I can help it."

"I don't much care what you want," she snapped back, and Jacob had to bite back a smile.

There she was.

And a sort of devilment awoke inside him. Angering her seemed dangerous and foolish, but it was better to bear the fire of her anger than deal with the iciness of her apathy.

"Well, it's my job to see you home safely, and the safest way to do that is privately."

She turned her head now, a renegade sable curl caught on her cheek, and Jacob itched to sweep it back. But he couldn't be sure his hand would survive the action, so he kept it clenched in a fist instead.

"If you think," she said through gritted teeth, "that I am getting into a coach *alone* with you for two days, you are very much mistaken."

Her palpable anger almost made him nostalgic.

"Princess, be reasonable. You will be far more comfortable in a private coach than squashed into a public one. I'm only thinking of your best interests."

That wasn't entirely true. He was thinking of having two days alone with her to plead his case and beg for her forgiveness.

But short of kidnapping her and throwing her bodily into a carriage, he couldn't force her to acquiesce.

They'd stopped outside the coaching inn, and Jacob

jumped lightly down from the gig, rushing around to her side, lest she stubbornly try to disembark herself.

He held up his arms and she scowled at him before sighing and allowing him to lift her down.

They were in the middle of a public courtyard in broad daylight, yet Jacob couldn't help but hold onto her even after her feet had touched the ground.

The feel of her pressed against him, the scent of her skin, and those heart-breaking eyes were too tempting, too precious to him.

Harriet pushed against his chest, but he refused to let her go until she glared up at him.

"Let me go," she spat.

"I will," he said softly. "But I have to tell you something first."

"I don't want to listen to anything you have to say," she threw back defiantly.

"Harriet, I hurt you. I was dishonest, and you have suffered for it, and I hate that. I can't change it, but I can try to explain. To make it up to you, somehow. If you'll let me."

Her expression hadn't changed, but he saw a flash of something in the deep brown depths of her eyes. Some intense emotion.

But in an instant, it was gone, and she merely looked angry again.

Jacob dropped his hands but kept her trapped between his body and the gig behind her.

"What is there to explain?" she demanded. "It's perfectly clear to me what happened. You were hired to take care of me like a big, overgrown nanny. And you lied about who you were."

"So did you," he interrupted gently. It was probably madness to argue with her, but he was desperate to get through this with her.

Harriet huffed out an impatient breath.

"My lie didn't hurt you, Jacob."

She spoke softly, and to his cravat, but her words cut him to the quick. Because she was right.

"I didn't mean to hurt you, sweetheart. I didn't mean for any of this to happen."

She looked at him then, right into his soul.

"You made me think that you—that we—"

Her cheeks grew furiously red, and to Jacob's horror, her eyes filled with tears.

She tried rapidly blinking them away, but one escaped and that lone drop falling down her smooth cheek ravaged him.

"Harriet." He reached out once more, clasping her upper arms and bending so he could look fully into her eyes, so she could see the sincerity in the depths of his own. "Everything that happened between us these last two weeks. Everything I've said. Everything I've done—has been the absolute truth. This started out as assignment—*you* started out as an assignment. But that changed."

She gazed at him, and he couldn't read anything in her expression.

"Please," he continued hoarsely. "You have to believe me. Harriet, I—"

"Your Highness?"

Jacob and Harriet both turned at the sound of a surprised, feminine voice.

He swore under his breath.

The last thing he needed right now was Harriet being recognised.

"Thank goodness, I found you."

A tall, elegant lady hurried over.

"Oh, no." Jacob turned back to see Harriet's face fall. "Althea Furberg."

"LADY ALTHEA."

Harriet stepped quickly away from Jacob, pulling her royal mask firmly into place.

The last thing she needed was Althea Furberg's prying eyes noticing anything going on between her and Jacob.

How the lady had ended up here in Gant, Harriet had no idea. But she was here now, and much as Harriet disliked her, she might just provide a solution to Harriet's current problem.

Namely, getting as far away from Jacob and the

temptation to fall back under his spell as possible. As quickly as possible.

"What has brought you to Gant?" She did her level best to keep her tone even, as though it wasn't at all odd for her to be alone with a strange man, dressed in a servant's cloak, and away from the palace.

"Why, I came to find you, Your Highness."

Harriet frowned in confusion as Lady Althea stepped closer still, lowering her voice conspiratorially.

"His Royal Highness sent me to get you," she whispered.

Harriet stared at the lady in amazement.

Just how many dratted minders had Christopher sent after her?

"H-he told me what happened."

The patronising, faintly disapproving look in Lady Althea's eyes made Harriet want to scratch them out.

"About how you had acted out when he was trying to keep you safe."

Harriet stiffened her shoulders.

Lady Althea's insubordination was grating enough, but the faux concern and sneery tone of voice were the outside of enough.

"My brother said those words to you, Lady Althea?" she asked, managing to look down her nose at the lady, even though she was a head shorter than the towering brunette.

Lady Althea had the grace to blush.

"Well," she hesitated. "He was just so terribly worried, Highness. You are, after all, the only princess. And Christopher—" she paused to twitter gratingly. "I mean, His Royal Highness, was quite beside himself."

Harriet didn't quite know what to make of this little speech.

Althea reached out a hand and placed it on Harriet's elbow as though they were close confidantes, ignoring Jacob completely.

"He wouldn't have betrayed such a scandalous secret to anyone else, I'm sure, Your Highness. But he knows how much I would worry. I have come to think of you as a sister of sorts. And I know your brother wouldn't have trusted anyone else to treat this situation with the delicacy it so clearly requires."

The barb behind Lady Althea's sycophantic words wasn't lost on Harriet. Her behaviour was scandalous. Shameful. Needed delicate handling.

And if Christopher had taken Althea into his confidences like that, it could only mean that he was planning on making the lady a part of the royal family. He would never discuss private family matters with the lady otherwise.

But if Christopher had sent Jacob to watch Harriet, why had he sent Althea now?

"Why don't we go and have a nice cup of tea?" Lady Althea spoke as though they were lifelong friends, and it was annoying in the extreme. "And I'll instruct the driver to prepare the horses."

"I don't think so."

Jacob's voice was pleasant enough, but Harriet heard the thread of steel in it, and she was sure Lady Althea could hear it, too.

Althea raised a brow at Jacob.

"And you are?" she sniffed.

"The Honourable Mr. Jacob Lauer, son of the Count of Dresbonne, at your service my lady."

Jacob was polite and gentlemanly, bowing to Lady Althea, but Harriet saw the glint of mischief in the blue depths of his eyes, and knew he was enjoying subtly putting the lady in her place.

"Oh, h-how nice to make your acquaintance, Mr. Lauer," Althea said weakly. "And what are you doing here with our dear Princess Harriet *alone*?"

Harriet heard the emphasis on the word *alone* and knew what Althea was implying; that there was something of an intimate nature between Harriet and Jacob.

The kicker was that Harriet had thought so, too. As it turned out, Jacob was just a consummate actor, and good at his job.

This sharp reminder of Harriet's foolishness and humiliation at Jacob's hands fuelled her resentment once more.

"I am escorting the princess back to the palace and to Prince Christopher," Jacob answered smoothly.

"And why is that? You just happened upon her, did you?" Althea sneered.

Jacob didn't answer, merely watched the lady closely.

"Well, I'm sure the princess will feel more comfortable in the company of a lady," Lady Althea said. "Someone she trusts."

Jacob's jaw clenched in reaction to Althea's words, and he turned his cobalt gaze on Harriet.

She knew, without him even speaking, that he was waiting for her to argue. To say she wanted to stay with him.

And because that was true, she needed to leave.

"Thank you, Mr. Lauer. But your assistance is no longer required," she mumbled miserably, refusing to meet his gaze. "Lady Althea is right. I would rather go with someone I trust."

She didn't look into his eyes, and she didn't give him a chance to respond.

Leaving her bags in the gig, Harriet simply turned and walked away.

Chapter Nineteen

"YOUR HIGHNESS, DO wake up. Honestly, I thought you'd be far more interesting company than this."

Harriet was roughly shaken awake, and she sat up with a jolt, wondering for a moment where she was.

It all came flooding back to her within seconds, however. And at the same time, Lady Althea's words registered.

Harriet could only stare in shock at the other woman's audacity.

"I beg your pardon?" she gasped.

Lady Althea smiled. But rather than it be the fawning smile she used in Court, and especially around Christopher, it was cold and calculated and didn't reach her eyes.

"What exactly is going on here?" Harriet demanded.

Something didn't feel right about this.

She looked out the carriage window, surprised to see that it was dark. Wherever they were, they'd been travelling for some time.

"Why, I'm taking you somewhere safe, Princess."

"I don't think so." Harriet sat up fully, wide awake now. "I'm going home."

"Not just yet, Your Highness. There is work to be done first."

Althea's tone sent a slither of apprehension down Harriet's spine.

"What is the meaning of this?" she asked, pleased that her voice sounded steady even if her heart was racing.

Immediately, Harriet's mind went to Jacob, and she wished he were here. Wished she'd never left him. Regardless of anything else that had gone on between them, she'd always felt safe.

"Don't worry, Your Highness," Althea said in lieu of answering Harriet's question. "Your cousin just needs to have a little chat with you."

Now Harriet was really confused.

"My cousin?" she repeated with a frown.

"Indeed."

"What cousin?" she asked in bewilderment.

"Why, the Duke of Tallenburg, of course."

"The Duke of—"

"Tallenburg."

"I know who he is," Harriet gritted out.

The cousin who'd inherited his title from Harriet's uncle. The cousin who had restarted an old feud in the Wesselbach family. The cousin with whom Christopher had been negotiating when the attempt was made to assassinate the king and queen, her parents.

"Why are you taking me to Augustus?" Harriet asked, her confusion growing by the second. "Why would Christopher send me to him?"

Althea's tinkling laugh grated on Harriet's already taut nerves. This was too much to deal with.

First, Jacob's betrayal and now this?

"Oh, Princess. You really don't understand the world around you, do you?"

Harriet only frowned.

Althea was older than her, true. But not by enough to be so terribly patronising.

"Augustus just needs to make sure that the prince will be more *amenable* to his requests."

"His requests?"

Harriet felt like an idiot and for a moment, her long-held resentment burst forth.

If Father, and Christopher, and even Alex hadn't treated her like a doll, an empty vessel who shouldn't know anything about the world around her, maybe she could guess at what Althea could mean.

Althea sighed.

"You really have no idea, do you? Augustus just wants to reason with *one* member of the royal family. I don't think it's too much to ask. When the assassination attempt on your father didn't create the distraction that he needed, we thought perhaps a simple trade agreement would suffice."

"We?" Harriet repeated, her mind spinning from everything Althea was revealing. "I don't understand. You and Christopher—I thought—"

"You thought that I was so desperately in love with your brother that I hung around him desperately hoping for a proposal," Althea said bluntly. "Well, you're not entirely wrong. In my youth, I would have done anything to marry your brother. And my parents certainly want it. But two years ago, I spent a summer in Tallenburg and met Augustus." Harriet was amazed to see a blush stain Lady Althea's cheeks. "In Aldonia, I might have been queen one day but with a man who would never truly care for me. But with Augustus— well, you haven't yet fallen in love, Princess. But when you do, you'll understand."

Harriet very much doubted it. For she had fallen in love, and she still didn't understand what was going on.

"Yet Christopher sent you to find me?"

Lady Althea smirked. "Not exactly. Ah, here we are."

The carriage drew to a stop and the door was opened before Harriet had time to catch her breath, let alone ask Lady Althea any more questions.

Standing before her was a tall, slender man with the

most chilling eyes Harriet had ever seen.

"Harriet. We meet at last."

"I assume you're my cousin?" Harriet made her voice as haughty as she could manage. "We might be related, but you are still only the duke of a small, insignificant duchy. You will address me as Your Highness."

That was only the second time in her entire life that Harriet had insisted someone use her title. And whereas she'd done it with Jacob to cover her hurt, now it was in an effort not to appear intimidated by this cold, dark stranger.

His black eyes flashed with anger, but he maintained the small, insincere smile nonetheless.

"Of course, Your Highness." He bowed deferentially, confusing Harriet even more.

Holding out a hand, he helped Lady Althea from the carriage first before turning to help Harriet.

Harriet didn't miss that while Althea gazed adoringly at the duke, he barely even glanced in her direction.

"And what am I doing here?" Harriet continued in the condescending tone she'd adopted. "And *where* exactly is here?"

"I will answer all of your questions, of course. I must assure you that you are not in any danger, Princess. As long as everything goes as it should, this whole business should be done with in a matter of days."

"This business being?"

His hand was still outstretched to assist her, but Harriet refused to move.

"The Royal family owns mines in Tallenburg, Princess Harriet. Very lucrative mines. My father bowed to pressure and refused to fight to get them back."

He smiled again, baring his teeth.

"I am not my father."

Harriet remembered talks of relations worsening with Tallenburg again. It was why Christopher had spent so much time away.

Clearly, negotiations had not gone well.

"So, this has what to do with me, exactly?"

"Nothing," he answered swiftly. "And you will be returned to the palace and the welcoming arms of your big brother." He sneered.

Suddenly, his expression changed, and Harriet recoiled slightly.

"Just as soon as he hands over the deeds to the mines."

Harriet's heart skipped a beat, and she wished quite desperately that Jacob were here.

"You mean—"

"I mean," he answered and this time, he reached in and pulled her bodily from the conveyance, only just stopping her from tumbling to the ground. "Prince Christopher has a decision to make. You or the mines."

JACOB SIGHED AS he extracted himself from the overly friendly hands of the serving wench in the inn at Gant.

He should have gone back to the palace the second Harriet left with that God-awful woman. He knew that.

Yet he'd sat here wallowing in self-pity all day and all evening.

Now, it was too late to travel anywhere, and he'd have to wait until tomorrow.

"If you're lonely, I don't mind keeping you company, sir."

The wench placed another tankard of ale on the table in front of Jacob, displaying her considerable assets with a distinct lack of shame.

Perhaps a few weeks ago he might have even taken her up on her less-than-subtle offer.

He'd always managed to enjoy himself on assignment before.

Perhaps, if he hadn't been ruined for every other female by a pair of huge brown eyes and a smart mouth, he'd be enjoying more than a tankard of ale right now.

But the truth was, he missed the princess who wanted nothing more to do with him. Missed the feel of her body against his, the touch of her lips, but more—he missed her witty mind and her sharp tongue and her mischievous laugh.

"She's ruined me," he muttered into his ale.

"What was that?"

He'd forgotten that the lady was awaiting some sort of answer.

Smiling in what he hoped was a polite and not at all flirtatious manner at the chit, he shook his head.

"I'm quite happy as I am, thank you."

Shrugging her shoulders and sending the top of her gown lower still, she moved off into the lap of a much more willing patron.

Jacob barely noticed.

Something was niggling at him about Harriet leaving with Lady Althea.

It wasn't just that he wanted to snatch her back and keep her with him.

Why would Prince Christopher send a lady to bring back his sister when he'd assigned Jacob to the task of taking care of her?

And why, when they'd been communicating through post left at the inn since Jacob had first informed the prince of where they were, had he sent someone without even a communication?

It didn't feel right.

An uneasiness clawed at Jacob.

He'd been so preoccupied with his feelings that he'd ignored his instincts.

And instinct told him that something was wrong

with this whole situation.

Night-time be damned.

He'd wasted enough time, and he wasn't going to waste any more.

He no longer wanted to wait until tomorrow, he just wanted to get the hell out of here. Back to the palace, and work to keep the princess safe.

Just as Jacob marched toward the door, it banged open and a messenger rushed in.

A messenger in the distinctive livery of the Royal Family.

Jacob rushed over to the man and without a word, took him by the arm and dragged him back outside.

The last thing Harriet's reputation needed was a furore around her being here. And if the locals began to question why a royal messenger was running around at this time of night, it wouldn't be long before gossip spread like wildfire.

"Unhand me, sir," the messenger, a mere boy, shouted.

Jacob let go of him as soon as they were outside in the relative privacy of the courtyard.

"Whatever message you have is for me," he said, urgency and a sense of foreboding making his voice harsh.

"I am to deliver this to—"

"To me," Jacob finished and bent to snatch the missive from the boy's hand.

Prince Christopher's insignia. Just as he'd thought.

Breaking the wax seal, Jacob unfolded the sheaf of paper, cursing as he read the contents.

Assassin apprehended. It was as we suspected. Bring her home.

Bring her home.

Jacob's entire body filled with icy dread.

Bring her home?

The prince hadn't sent Lady Althea to retrieve Harriet.

And if she'd known to come here, that meant she was the informant in the palace.

They'd always known, or at least suspected, that Tallenburg was behind the attempt. It made sense.

He was mercenary in the extreme and driven by a vendetta against the Wesselbachs that went back a century.

The assassination would have been an attempt to throw Aldonia into chaos, force Prince Christopher to focus more on the politics of home and less on the lucrative business interests of the royal family in Tallenburg.

But they hadn't been able to figure out how the duke was getting his information before Jacob had been sent after Princess Harriet.

But now he knew—it was Althea Furberg. And he also knew that Prince Christopher could have no idea, for he hadn't mentioned it.

"I need a fast horse," he said to the messenger, who was standing mutely beside him. Jacob knew the gelding he'd bought from the farmer would be less than useless at anything more than a slow trot.

The young man merely stared back.

"Where's your horse, dammit?" Jacob yelled.

He knew he needed to calm down. Knew he was on the verge of panic.

But he couldn't help himself.

Lady Althea was obviously in league with the duke. And they had Harriet.

Chapter Twenty

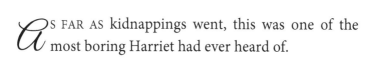

$\mathcal{A}$S FAR AS kidnappings went, this was one of the most boring Harriet had ever heard of.

Her cousin, the duke, was a disappointing villain. In all of Harriet's gothic novels there were tales of debauchery, and sword fights, and crazed men locking poor, unsuspecting heroines up left and right.

But this? This was nothing like that.

Her cousin was treating her—well, like royalty.

She wasn't locked in a tower. She wasn't being starved or beaten or left in a dank dungeon.

In fact, if she wasn't here against her will, and if she didn't have to suffer the company of her cousin and the traitorous Lady Althea, it might be quite pleasant.

There was, however, the small matter of her being unable to leave.

Augustus had guards around both the modest country house in which she was being kept and the rather sizeable grounds.

He'd informed Harriet during one of the dinners he forced her to attend that the house had been a recent purchase. A base from which to carry out his plan.

She wasn't allowed out onto the grounds. She wasn't allowed to even spend more than a few minutes alone.

Even now, she only had this time to herself because she'd dashed to the library when Lady Althea wasn't looking and had been hiding behind a heavy brocade curtain ever since.

But Althea would find her, of course.

Harriet felt a now-familiar spurt of anger when she thought of the other lady.

She'd never wanted Christopher to marry Althea. She'd never thought the statuesque woman was good for Christopher.

But what if he'd loved her? He wasn't given to displays of emotion, but still—he'd trusted her, of that Harriet was certain.

Althea had spent days now bragging to Harriet about how she'd managed to get information of Harriet's whereabouts from the prince.

It would appear that the lady had moved from simply sending messages to her lover, to blatantly stealing Christopher's private correspondence.

Which is how she'd found out about Harriet's presence here.

Harriet knew she should be worried about her safety.

She knew she should be worried about relations between Aldonia and Tallenburg, and how far her cousin would go to get what he wanted.

But now that she knew her family was relatively safe, she couldn't help but worry more about Christopher than anything else.

Had his heart been engaged with Lady Althea? Would he be heartbroken?

With Alex happily married, was it the destiny of the other two siblings to be miserable when it came to love?

Christopher had been about to propose to Althea—a lady who betrayed him, not only as a man but as a prince.

And Harriet—Harriet had had her heart broken by a man who had pretended to care for her just so he could stay close and do his job.

A white-hot anger, swift and furious suddenly rose up in her.

Anger was better than sadness. Gritted teeth better than tears.

How *dare* ghastly Althea Furberg treat Christopher thusly? Harriet simply wouldn't stand for it.

Althea had such grand plans. She hung on Augustus' every word, convinced that Christopher would immediately hand over the deeds to every mine

Aldonia owned in Tallenburg. Convinced that she and Augustus would run off together and be blissfully happy spending Aldonian money in Tallenburg.

Well, Harriet simply wouldn't allow it.

Was she furious at Jacob? Absolutely. But her feelings toward him were too difficult to confront right now. And so she focused all her anger on Althea Furberg and what she had done to Christopher.

The door to the library suddenly sprung open and, releasing a sigh, Harriet stepped out from behind the curtain. It wouldn't take Althea long to find her, so there was little point in hiding.

"Ah, Your Highness. There you are."

Althea had been like Harriet's shadow for four days now and if the grimace on the lady's face was anything to go by, she was as happy about that as Harriet was.

"You do rise with the birds, don't you?"

Harriet merely scowled at her.

She worried that Lady Althea was quite mad. All day, she twittered away to Harriet as though they were the closest of friends on a luxurious sojourn in the country.

See? Harriet told herself. *The worst kidnapping ever.*

"Your cousin has requested your company at breakfast, Princess."

Harriet didn't miss the slight bite in Althea's tone.

That was another thing she'd noticed over the last few days. That while Lady Althea hung on Augustus' every word, he spent all of his time ingratiating himself to Harriet, and Althea was not happy about it.

Well, Harriet decided as she followed Althea from the room, she was done being a pawn in Tallenburg's game with her brother.

She wasn't going to sit around here waiting for Christopher to send in the guard, which he would, just as soon as he received Tallenburg's letter.

The duke thought Christopher would be so scandal adverse that he would happily hand over the mine deeds for Harriet's safe and secret return.

But he didn't know Christopher.

He might be subtle. And sometimes overly concerned with reputation and public appearance.

But he had a core of steel and would not give in to blackmail. That's why he would make a wonderful king. Why he was already running Aldonia.

The ladies swept into the ostentatious formal dining room and took their seats, either side of where the duke would sit at the head, as though he were sitting on a throne.

The duke had delusions of grandeur and an unhealthy obsession with wealth. It would, Harriet was sure, be his downfall.

And she wasn't going to sit around waiting to be used in his dastardly scheme.

She was getting out of there the very first chance she got.

"HE'LL BE EXPECTING capitulation, of that there is no doubt."

"Indeed. And an answer soon."

Jacob stood from the table at which he, Prince Christopher, Prince Alexander, and Hans were discussing the situation.

The situation.

That's what Prince Christopher had called his sister being bloody well kidnapped.

After Jacob had burst through the palace gates as though the hounds of Hell were chasing him and demanded to see the prince, it hadn't taken them long to figure things out.

Knowing that Lady Althea was Tallenburg's informant must have been a blow to Prince Christopher. Everyone who worked for the palace, or who attended court, had assumed there would be an announcement soon.

Yet the man had been stoic, caring only that the princess be returned safely and without scandal.

The Furbergs had been questioned, but nothing had come of that except hysterics from the mother who had thought her daughter would be queen.

For three days they'd investigated before finally discovering the property not far from Gant that had been bought by the duke using an alias.

In the furore, nobody had made comment on the fact that the princess had been taken on Jacob's watch. But once they got her back, he knew a reckoning was coming.

And he deserved it.

But he didn't give a damn about his job. About the interrogation that was sure to come. About the uncomfortable questions he'd be forced to answer.

All he cared about was Harriet. He wanted her back. Safely in his arms, even though she probably still hated him.

She could hate him, though. Just as long as she was safe while doing it.

"We've done enough talking," He tried and failed to keep his tone even.

And he knew by the shrewd look of both princes and the shaking of Hans's head, that he was making his feelings more than obvious.

"I just—" He swallowed a sudden lump in his throat. "I know that I am responsible. I let the princess go."

"And we will get her back."

This came from Prince Alexander, who had arrived at the palace while Jacob and Harriet had been in the cottage. It seemed like a lifetime ago now.

And while the younger prince was a lot more laid back than his older brother, there was no denying the fact that he was worried about his sister and wanted her safely returned.

He'd also been watching Jacob closely for the last few days. Jacob didn't know what the prince was looking for. All he knew was that it made him nervous.

Prince Christopher had given no outward reaction to either the news that Harriet was gone, or that his intended was behind the kidnapping.

He'd merely listened quietly to Jacob's panicked ramblings before calling for Prince Alexander, and then Hans.

Now they'd finally arrived at an inn near Tallenburg's property, and instead of storming in there and grabbing Harriet, they were *still* sitting here discussing strategy.

"Not by sitting here twiddling our thumbs, we won't," he snapped before he even realised what he was doing.

But, hang it. He didn't care about propriety or respect. Not when Harriet was trapped with that bastard Tallenburg.

There was a moment of shocked silence before he groaned and dropped his head in his hands. Prince Christopher's black eyes narrowed, and Prince Alexander suddenly burst into laughter.

"Mr. Lauer." He smirked, seeming completely uncaring about Jacob's insubordination. "I think once Harriet is back, we should have a talk you and I."

Jacob's cravat suddenly felt like a noose around his neck, but he resisted the urge to pull at it tellingly.

"Before we get into that," Prince Christopher said now, his tone low and calm as always. "And we *will* be getting into that—" His eyes flashed to Jacob's, and there was that damned tightening in his cravat once more. "I need to decide what we're doing."

Jacob sat back down reluctantly, drumming his fingers impatiently on the well-scrubbed wooden table around which they sat.

"Tallenburg is expecting a reply from me. I think our best option is to send him a letter agreeing to meet. If he thinks he's got the upper hand, it may make him overly confident."

"And what?" Jacob interrupted. "Allow him to use Harr—I mean, the princess, as bait? He could hurt her. He could have *already* hurt her."

Jacob's stomach roiled at the idea, and the murderous feeling that had plagued him for the past few nights took hold once more.

"He won't hurt her." Prince Christopher sounded far too relaxed for Jacob's liking. Though when he looked up, both he and Prince Alexander were wearing matching, grim expressions.

Nobody in this room knew what the duke was capable of. And that scared Jacob witless.

"When you meet, what then?" Prince Alexander asked. "He's hardly going to hand Harriet over to us without first having his hands on the deeds."

Prince Christopher smiled suddenly.

"No, he won't," he agreed. "Because Harriet won't be there."

Jacob was pleased to see that both Hans and Prince Alexander looked as confused as he felt.

"Where will she be?" the younger prince asked.

"If I write to Tallenburg today agreeing to an exchange, he'll make sure that not a hair on Harriet's head is touched," Prince Christopher said. "The agreement is a guarantee that she'll be kept safe."

"All right," Prince Alexander nodded. "I still don't understand."

"I'll arrange a meeting for tomorrow," Prince Christopher continued, "And we will be taking Harriet tonight."

Jacob's eyes snapped up to the prince's.

"Yes," he whispered his approval of the plan without even realising.

"A stealth recovery of the princess?" Hans spoke for the first time. "Forgive me, Your Royal Highness, but two agents and two princes of the realm don't exactly make for a subtle operation."

"Indeed." Prince Christopher gave the ghost of a smile. "That's why only one of us is going in."

"Me."

Jacob had jumped to his feet, his chair clattering on the flagstone floor of the private dining room in the process.

Once more the princes exchanged a look.

"No," Prince Christopher said, shocking Jacob. "You are—too close to it."

His words let Jacob know, in no uncertain terms, that he knew this was way, way more than an assignment to Jacob.

"Mr. Maylt, will—"

"No."

Jacob's objection brought a shocked cessation to the conversation.

But he was past caring.

When the full story of the last couple of weeks came out, he'd be exiled from Aldonia anyway. And nothing—not king, not country—would stop him from getting to the woman he loved.

"My apologies, Your Royal Highness," he said, even though he wasn't a bit sorry. "I have no wish to countermand your orders."

He took a deep breath, knowing that he was about to confirm all the unspoken suspicions floating around the room. "But if you don't send me in to get the princess, I'll go in myself, either way."

Prince Christopher slowly came to his feet, followed by Prince Alexander, and finally Hans, who was staring at Jacob as though he'd run mad.

Prince Christopher stared at Jacob, and Jacob stared right back. Refusing to back down. Refusing to show any sort of weakness in his position.

The prince looked to his brother, who gave an almost imperceptible nod.

Finally, he looked back at Jacob.

"Well then." The Crown Prince gave Jacob a look that seemed to go beyond that of a leader giving orders. Suddenly, he didn't look like the leader of a country facing a crisis. He looked like a big brother worried about his sister. "Go get the princess."

Chapter Twenty-One

"YOU CAN DO this, Harriet. You didn't think you could run away by yourself, and look what happened."

Even though she was whispering to herself like a madwoman, she still feared that someone would hear her.

Yes, look what happened, a voice in her head piped up. *You didn't even get out of the palace alone. And Christopher knew. The entire time.*

Right, well that was a bad example of her capabilities perhaps. But *this*—this she could do.

Harriet took a steadying breath then leaned out the open window to peer at the ground below.

It seemed a very long way down. And the tree that she was planning to use for her escape seemed a lot further away now in the dark of night than it had been earlier.

But time was wasting. She knew it wouldn't be long

before a maid was sent to check on her, ostensibly to see if she required anything before she retired to bed for the night.

It was a small window of opportunity she had. And she needed to take it or be used by Tallenburg in his dastardly scheme.

The man had been salivating over Christopher's letter earlier. A letter in which Christopher had agreed to meet to discuss the exchange.

Harriet's anger had burst forth as Augustus had crowed and Althea had fawned over him as though he were a god and not a petty, jealous little man.

She wanted to scratch Althea's eyes out.

Instead, she'd pleaded a headache and retired to her rooms.

A stiff breeze caught her stolen, dark servant's cloak and sent it billowing about her shoulders.

Harriet pulled it closer. The dull cloak was imperative to her plan. Should any guard catch sight of the ivory silk that Lady Althea had insisted on lending her, even though it was far too long, it would be like a beacon to the guards patrolling the gardens.

If she could stay hidden beneath the voluminous cloak however, she could get herself to the walls at least. And hopefully a gate that led out of the grounds.

Donning the cloak again had brought all sorts of memories rushing back to Harriet, and she'd found herself missing Jacob so much that the feeling was an acute pain.

She didn't *want* to miss him. She didn't *want* to remember that he'd held her, and kissed her, and told her that she was brave and capable of anything. But her foolish heart wouldn't be reasoned with.

The clock on the mantle chimed the hour, and Harriet knew her time was fast running out.

She'd have to reach out as far as she could, grab hold of the closest tree limb then swing herself into the branches.

She'd either survive or fall to her death.

If she did fall, her parents and her brothers would be devastated. The country would be plunged into chaos.

She didn't want to think about whether Jacob would care or not, fearing that the answer would be too painful.

A small cluster of clouds that had been somewhat blocking the moon moved, and suddenly the tree and the grounds were illuminated by the coldly bright moonlight.

Not giving herself any more time to wonder if she were mad, Harriet stepped onto the window ledge and reached toward the branch with one hand, the other clasping the window frame in a deathlike grip.

Her fingers grazed the coarse surface of the tree branch, not quite gaining purchase.

Harriet stretched further still.

Just a tiny bit more…

Suddenly, she lost her grip on the window frame and tipped forward.

At the last moment, her hand wrapped fully round the limb of the tree and she swung her other arm up to grip it.

Gasping in fright, Harriet hung for a heart-stopping moment before a survival instinct kicked in and she swung herself toward the relative safety of the tree trunk.

She almost wept with relief as her feet found purchase on a sturdy branch.

With her heart hammering loudly enough to be heard across the grounds, she scrambled further inward until she was pressed flush against the tree trunk.

Her eyes were smarting and her breath was heaving.

But she'd done it!

This time, she'd really done it alone. With no help from Jacob, or Christopher, or Alex, or anybody.

It had been ungainly and undignified. But ultimately successful.

Now, to get her feet on solid ground.

The process was long and arduous.

Her cloak and hair snagged in twig after twig. Her skirts caught and she winced as she heard more than one tearing sound.

And her hands, she knew, were covered in scrapes and scratches.

But finally, after an age, Harriet got to the lowest branch and with one steadying breath, she jumped and landed with only a whispered "oomph" onto the blessedly sturdy ground below.

Harriet bent forward, clasping her knees and dragging some much-needed oxygen into her burning lungs.

She glanced up at the tree, hardly daring to believe that she'd managed to get down it. That she was free.

She straightened up, pulling the hood of the cloak over her head and preparing to run across the grounds.

Suddenly, a hand clamped around her mouth, another dragged her back against a large, rock solid body.

Her attempts to scream froze and died in her throat as a familiar voice whispered furiously in her ear, the breath tickling her neck and sending gooseflesh all over her body.

"I swear," the voice growled. "If I ever catch you jumping out of windows and climbing down trees again, I will lock you in a tower, so help me God."

The hand from her mouth dropped to her shoulder, spinning her around to face Jacob's furious glare.

"What—"

Before she could speak another word, he pulled her close and bent his head, capturing her mouth in a ferocious kiss, and sending her thoughts skittering on the wind.

HE HADN'T MEANT to kiss her.

Of course, he hadn't.

This was neither the time nor the place.

Yet when he'd spied her, hanging from a bloody window, Jacob had never felt fear like it.

He'd been all set to get inside the house, get Harriet, and get out within thirty minutes. Maybe an hour, allowing for any potential run-ins with Tallenburg's guards.

Yet he'd stood at the base of that tree, unable to do anything other than watch in sickening apprehension, for eons.

When she'd lost her grip on the damned window frame, he'd felt his legs give way and only sheer force of will had kept him upright, his eyes fixed on the beautiful, brave, *insane* woman scrambling for purchase on the bloody tree.

Jacob had prayed, cursed, barely breathed, and almost cast up his accounts as he watched helplessly from the ground.

The relief he'd felt when she'd reached the base had made him so light-headed, the world had actually spun for a moment before his anger, swift and fiery, had refocused his mind.

Pulling her against him, he'd only intended to make her aware of his presence, to blister her ears for her folly, to assure himself that she was safe and real and in his arms.

But the scent of her had teased his nostrils, and the feel of her soft, delectable curves, even through the voluminous cloak, had reminded him of all those days they'd spent together. It had been like an oasis in a desert to a man dying of thirst.

And so, trembling with the remnants of fear as well as the desperate need that only she could evoke, he'd turned her in his arms and drunk his fill.

And now, instead of getting her to safety, he was kissing the living daylights out of her on enemy territory.

The stark reminder that she was still in danger dragged Jacob's mind from the gutter in which it had planted itself and back firmly on the task at hand.

Pulling his lips from hers, he gazed down into her face, awaiting the moment that she'd open those eyes and he'd fall into them all over again.

He studied her face for any signs of injury or distress. But, he thought rather smugly, she looked nothing other than beautiful and thoroughly kissed.

Jacob allowed himself a moment of unadulterated male pride as he took in the blush on her satiny smooth cheeks that was visible even in the moonlight.

Her eyes fluttered, the lashes batting open.

He expected wonder. Awe. Desire, certainly. Maybe even a tear for the romance of it all.

But as he gazed into the deep brown pools of her eyes, they narrowed menacingly and he got the distinct impression that he was in trouble.

"Harriet," he whispered.

He didn't get to finish whatever it was he was going to stay.

Without warning, her boot-clad foot came down hard on the tip of his Hessian, causing him to curse profusely, though quietly, as pain radiated through his toes.

"What are you doing here?" she spat.

He gazed at her in affronted amazement before his temper rose to match her own.

"I'm rescuing you," he spat right back.

Her brow rose in superior disbelief, making him feel like an imbecile.

"Oh really?" she sneered. "Thank goodness you were here to watch me climb down a tree. However would I have managed without you?"

Jacob rolled his eyes at her sarcasm.

"If you would have just waited for someone to rescue you, you wouldn't have had to climb down the damned tree," he bit out, uncaring that he was swearing at the Crown Princess.

"Well, four days seemed long enough for a supposed elite agent of the Crown to manage to enter *one* house to rescue *one* person, so forgive me if I wasn't in the mood to wait."

"I didn't know you were here until yesterday," he shot at her, annoyed and embarrassed by her singularly low opinion of him. "And when I found out, I came as quickly as I could to—"

"To watch me rescue myself," she interrupted, her voice saccharine sweet. "My hero," she drawled sarcastically.

"You are the most ill-mannered, ungrateful person I've ever rescued," he sniffed, mortally wounded by her attitude.

Her jaw dropped as she scowled furiously up at him.

"You *haven't* rescued me," she screeched even in a whisper which, he grudgingly had to admit, was rather impressive. He could only imagine the volume would make his ears bleed if she were free to yell.

"And you're not going to," she continued, her chest heaving with outrage. "You might have tricked me into allowing you to interfere with my getaway, Jacob Lauer. But you will *not* stop me from rescuing myself. Now, get out of my way."

She made to stomp past him, but Jacob shot out a hand and clasped her upper arm, gently but firmly.

He was not going to allow her to mess up her own

rescue. It was as simple as that.

"What do you think you're doing?" she demanded, every inch the princess. "Unhand me at once."

"No," he said simply, preparing for her outrage.

"You – I – you – how dare you?" she spluttered, pulling against his hold. All she managed to do was tire herself out.

"Let's just get out of here." He tried to coax her into being agreeable, at least until they got to safety.

"I'm not going with you," she insisted, and the mutinous set to her lips told him that she was serious. "My brother—"

"Your brother is waiting at a safe place nearby for me to bring you back," he interrupted. "They both are."

She frowned then blinked in surprise.

"Alex is here?"

"Yes. He is," he said evenly. "And both of your brothers want you out of here safely, just as much as I do."

"Christopher sent you."

Was it Jacob's imagination, or did she sound ever so slightly disappointed?

"Well, tell him thank you, but I can find my own way out of this without interference from him, or you, or anybody else."

Jacob closed his eyes and prayed for patience.

She would turn his hair white before he got her the hell out of here.

"I can't do that," he said through gritted teeth.

"Why not?" she demanded.

"Because," he snapped, his temper fraying. "He didn't want me to be the one rescuing you in the first place, and if I go back without you, he'll very likely put a bullet in me."

"Oh," was all she said, but Jacob could practically see the wheels turning in that baffling head of hers. Then she frowned.

"Why didn't he want you rescuing me?"

They really didn't have the time to be standing here discussing this.

Yet Jacob couldn't resist the opportunity to talk to her without her yelling at him or worse, crying over him.

He laughed, but it was a harsh and humourless sound.

"Because," he said dully. "I'm the reason you're here in the first place. I was supposed to be protecting you, Harriet. Not—" He swallowed past a lump in his throat. "Not seducing you and hurting you. Sending you off straight into the enemy's clutches."

She was quiet for an age, and Jacob found himself desperately wondering what she was thinking.

"It's not your fault," she finally mumbled grudgingly. "I chose to leave with Althea. I wouldn't let you take me home."

"You chose to go because of me. You know it. I

know it. And the prince knows it."

"But you're here," she said, a look of consternation and something he couldn't quite decipher lighting her eyes.

"Yes, I am."

"So, he changed his mind?"

"I can't say that I gave him much of a choice," Jacob answered.

He knew what she was thinking; Prince Christopher's choice was the only choice.

Jacob had a decision to make. He could try to charm her, coax her, distract her from her questions.

Or he could come clean. Tell her the truth, even though it wouldn't make a difference.

"The prince knew I would have come anyway, Harriet. Regardless of whether he allowed it or not."

"And disobey his orders?" She frowned. "Why on earth would you do that?"

Jacob took a steadying breath and looked straight into her eyes, the eyes that had haunted his dreams for the past four nights.

"Because I needed to be the one to make you safe," he said. "Because I wanted to be here with you. Because I never wanted to be parted from you in the first place."

He stepped closer until nothing was separating them, until she had to tilt her head to look up and see the sincerity of his words in his face.

"Because," he said softly. "I love you."

Chapter Twenty-Two

"*W*ELL, ISN'T THIS cosy?"

Before Harriet's world even began to right itself after Jacob's words, another voice sounded in the darkness, and she found herself being moved, quick as a flash, until she was standing behind Jacob.

He was facing away from her, his shoulders tense, all of his focus on the duke, who was strolling toward them.

His appearance wasn't enough to frighten Harriet.

The revolver he had trained on them, however, was a different matter.

"Now, see what you've done?" she whispered furiously to Jacob's back, since it was the only part of him she could currently see.

"What *I've* done?" He sounded incredulous and furious, though he still didn't turn around. "We would have been out of here if you had just, for once, done what you were told."

Harriet hadn't forgotten what he'd said only minutes ago. The words were embedded in her head, as bright and fantastical as the fireworks they lit at the palace on every royal birthday and occasion.

And she couldn't even begin to process how she felt about them.

He loved her. He loved her!

And she loved him, too. Desperately.

In spite of the hurt, the anger, the sense of betrayal. She loved him.

But right now, she could happily wring his neck.

And truth be told, it sounded as though the feeling was mutual.

What sort of person professed his love for a lady and then proceeded to berate her?

"If I had done what I was told? Who are you to order me about?" she demanded hotly. "I was managing just fine without you. Yet still, you felt the need to swan in here and then *kiss* me as though we had time for that, and now—"

"Silence!"

Harriet had quite forgotten her cousin was there.

She peeked out from behind Jacob's oversized shoulder to see Augustus staring at them both as though they should be in a lunatic asylum.

"Now, I'd like to know what you're doing here, Mr.—?"

Harriet wondered how Jacob would handle the

situation.

Would he pull a weapon of his own? Reason with her captor?

But, no. To her amazement, he held a hand up to Augustus as though the gun in the man's hand were of no significance.

"Hold on a minute," he told her cousin, who stared at him, jaw agape.

In the next instant Jacob had turned to face her, his face a mask of barely bridled fury.

"I kissed you because I love you, you impossible woman. And I have never felt a fear like what I've felt with you gone. Even when I didn't know you were in danger, I was miserable. It felt as though my very soul had left my body when you walked away."

Harriet's heart stuttered at his words.

She searched his shockingly blue eyes for a trace of subterfuge, but all she saw was a blazing blue fire. A fire that set off an answering blaze in her.

"Turn back around at once."

The duke's jarring, nasally voice interrupted Harriet's thoughts.

With a frown of irritation, she leaned around Jacob.

"Oh, hush, Augustus," she snapped. "This is important."

"But the assignment—" she began, hardly daring to believe what he said.

"The assignment was just that. An assignment. Something I wasn't particularly happy about. And on the first day, I *still* wasn't particularly happy about it. But every day, every second since then were the happiest of my life."

"Jacob." Harriet felt her eyes fill as her feelings overwhelmed her.

This was the most romantic—

The distinctive sound of a revolver being prepared for firing interrupted her thoughts. And the moment.

"This is all very touching," Augustus said sarcastically. "But I'm afraid my cousin is needed. So, if you'll be so kind as to come with me? I'd hate to have to kill you."

Jacob rolled his eyes as though the threat of bodily harm were a mere inconvenience.

He turned to face Augustus. Harriet barely saw him move. Hardly heard a sound.

Yet within a split second, Augustus screamed in agony, and his revolver clattered to the ground.

He clutched his hand as he dropped to his knees, and Harriet was amazed to see a small, silver dagger protruding from the flesh.

"Did you—?" She gaped in awe.

"Well, he wouldn't stop talking and making threats," Jacob answered, sounding defensive.

"Harriet." He stepped closer, his arms reaching for her. "There are things we must discuss. Obstacles in our way. And I know this cannot come to anything. But—"

A sudden burst of sound and light rent the air as Tallenburg's guards came rushing toward them.

"Bloody hell, can't a man get a word out around here?" Jacob bellowed before turning to face the charge. "Get inside and stay there until I come for you," he said urgently.

Harriet opened her mouth to object to his harshly given orders.

But then he turned to look at her.

"Please, love," he said softly, his eyes tender and pleading.

Without another word, Harriet nodded then ran toward the house.

Outside she heard shouts, clashes of blades, and even a shot or two.

It sounded almost as chaotic out there as she felt inside after Jacob's wonderful words.

Almost, but not quite.

JACOB MADE LIGHT work of Tallenburg's first wave of guards.

By the time the next group of guards arrived, he'd been joined by Hans and the two princes who, he was pleased to see, were exceptionally skilled as swordsmen and pugilists.

Prince Christopher seemed to take great delight in dragging his cousin inside once the fighting had ceased.

And Prince Alexander looked like a child with a new toy as he rounded up fallen soldiers, in various states of ill-health, locking them up in a drawing room until the aid that Hans left to acquire arrived.

This particular incident would take an age to clean up, Jacob knew.

Relations between the Tallenburg duchy and the Aldonian crown would take no small amount of delicacy to sort out.

Thankfully, Prince Christopher said over the furious swearing and empty threats from his cousin, the younger Tallenburg seemed imminently more sensible than the elder.

Jacob had watched the prince carefully while Lady Althea made a spectacle of herself. First throwing herself at the apprehended duke, wailing and declaring her love in a most embarrassing fashion.

When the man dismissed her and her face paled dramatically—no doubt as the reality of her situation sank in—she threw herself at the prince, this time begging for mercy and claiming innocence.

The prince however, barely flinched in the face of such a vulgar and emotional display.

Jacob was quite sure that even if the man had intended to wed Lady Althea, his heart hadn't been involved in the decision, and it certainly wasn't affected now.

When the magistrate arrived with a bevy of men to assist, the prince ordered the lady be taken away with the rest of the prisoners, impervious to her caterwauling and the obvious discomfort of the portly magistrate.

All that was left now was for a carriage to be prepared. Something Prince Alexander ordered Tallenburg's household staff to do at once.

"He tried to use our sister as a piece of property to be traded," the prince said. "The least we can do is steal a carriage and a few horses. Oh, and—" He signalled to a footman, who seemed as dazed and shocked as the rest of the servants. "We'll also steal whatever you can pack up from the kitchens. And the wine cellar," he finished.

When the room emptied of everyone but the princes, Hans, Jacob, and Harriet, a stilted silence fell.

Jacob had so much he wanted to say. So much he wanted to do. Namely, take Harriet in his arms and never let her go.

But hell would freeze over before he'd ever get that opportunity again.

He knew it. And yet he could not regret that he'd confessed his feelings. Could not regret the love he'd discovered with her, and the short time they spent together.

Even though the hurt it caused now was almost killing him.

If he'd never loved the princess, he'd have been spared this pain.

Yet he would endure it for the happy times he'd known with her.

Prince Christopher stepped toward the princess, bending to speak swiftly in her ear. She nodded once, and he reached out and pulled her into a tight, short hug.

Next, Prince Alexander stepped forward and hugged her more freely but just as fiercely.

Jacob wanted so much to be the next to take her in his arms, yet he kept his distance. For what else could he do?

A footman arrived to inform His Royal Highness that the carriage was prepared, as was the food, as requested by His Highness.

"Come, Harriet." Prince Alexander took Harriet's hand and placed it in the crook of his arm. "I cannot wait to get back to Chillington Abbey and tell Lydia all about this. It's like something from one of her books."

Jacob watched helplessly as she was swept from the room with only the briefest of glances in his direction.

"Gentlemen, I would like to close out this matter as soon as possible. Mr. Maylt, can I trust that you will remain here and take care of this? I'll see you in my office in two weeks hence to discuss any loose ends."

Hans dutifully nodded.

The prince turned and walked swiftly to the door.

Before he stepped through it, however, he turned and looked directly at Jacob, his expression guarded and watchful.

"Lauer, I'd like to speak to you alone. Once you can leave this in Maylt's hands, see me directly. At the palace."

It wasn't a request, yet Jacob nodded all the same.

He'd known when he'd insisted on being the one to rescue the princess that he was opening himself up to this.

He didn't regret it, however.

Though arguing in the garden in the middle of her rescue hadn't exactly been his plan, Harriet was safe.

And at least he'd gotten to kiss her one last time.

Chapter Twenty-Three

———⟡———

$\mathcal{H}$ARRIET STOOD IN her favourite spot of the palace, watching the goings on of palace life through the glass of her tunnel.

The courtyard was bustling as it ever was.

And there were Mother and Father, safely strolling in their garden once more.

Christopher would be in his office, she knew.

And Alex had left just that morning for the docks, anxious to get back to Lydia in time to see the babe.

Harriet had promised to come and stay just as soon as news arrived of the baby. She didn't mind travelling to see them as long as it was of her own free will!

"Your Highness," Ansel's voice sounded behind her. "Here you are again."

Harriet turned slightly to smile at the butler before turning her attention to the courtyard once more.

She knew that Ansel was growing concerned for her. It was evident in his constant presence, and in the gentle tone he had taken to using when speaking to her.

"I'll leave shortly, Ansel," she assured him without turning back. "I'm just—"

A flash of movement caught her eye, and she looked to the side.

There he was.

Jacob strode purposefully through the courtyard, his blonde hair glinting in the spring sunshine, even under the beaver hat atop his head.

Her mind flashed back to when she'd been a girl and she'd watched him arrive late to military training.

Who would ever have thought that their paths would lead them back to each other, and then away again?

It was Fate. But it was cruel.

Jacob was an agent for Christopher. It was his job to travel throughout Europe, and possibly further, at the prince's bidding.

And even if he wasn't, he was the second son of the Count of Dresbonne. A good family name, but not an heir. Her father would never agree to a match.

Could Harriet do what her aunt had done before her? Give all of this up to be with the man she loved?

Already she knew the answer was a resounding yes.

Never had she been happier than those short, blissful weeks she'd spent with him in her tumbledown cottage. She knew that she could live anywhere, be anywhere, and be happy. As long as she was with him.

But they'd been home some days now, and this was the first she'd seen of him.

If he'd wanted to marry her, wouldn't he have come to her?

If he loved her as he said he did, wouldn't he have asked her to be his?

Jacob was nearing the edge of the courtyard, and Harriet resisted the urge to press her face against the glass, all the better to see him.

It wouldn't do, she knew, for the Crown Princess to be pressing herself against windowpanes.

Before he stepped through the doors leading to the royal offices, however, Jacob stopped.

He spun around and looked up at her tunnel of glass, his eyes searching until they found her.

Taking off his hat, he bowed low, that irresistible grin lighting his face. Yet even from this distance, Harriet could see a sadness behind the expression.

Before she could react, he was gone.

"AH, LAUER. HAVE things progressed sufficiently with Tallenburg?"

Jacob struggled to get his mind on the meeting at hand and away from the solitary figure of Princess Harriet, clad in pink, standing in the window.

Even from a distance, her beauty had taken his breath away.

Being this close to her, yet so far away in every way that mattered, was torture.

And Jacob wanted, quite desperately, to get away.

"Hans has things well in hand, Your Royal Highness," he answered, taking a seat when the prince resumed his behind the oak desk.

"I'm glad that we've managed to keep it relatively under wraps," the prince said. "The Furbergs will keep their title, and Althea will avoid gaol. I think that should be enough incentive for them to remain discreet."

Once more, Jacob was amazed by the prince's stoicism.

If he'd discovered that Harriet had betrayed him in such a way, he'd have been destroyed.

Yet Prince Christopher spoke as though the lady were nothing more than a troublesome stranger.

"I expect that Hans will be done by week's end, Prince Christopher. And no doubt ready for his next assignment."

"That brings me to *your* next assignment."

Jacob's heart thumped heavily, yet outwardly he remained calm.

He wanted this, he reminded himself. He wanted to be sent away from the agony of being close to Harriet and not able to make her his wife.

"So soon," he managed to say when the prince remained quiet. Watchful.

"I'm afraid the matter is something of a delicate nature." The prince leaned back, steepling his fingers and regarding Jacob with an assessing, black gaze.

A delicate nature.

That was how he'd referred to the assignment of protecting Harriet.

Jacob couldn't even claim he'd done a good job of that.

Yet, if the prince were already assigning him something else, he clearly didn't hold Jacob's behaviour against him.

Truth be told, he had thought he'd be coming here to answer deuced uncomfortable questions and then be thrown out on his arse.

"Forgive me, Highness," Jacob said. "I thought that perhaps, after Gant. After the princess," he prevaricated slightly before deciding that bluntness was his best option. "To be frank, I wasn't sure if you'd trust me with a delicate matter."

"Yes, well as to that, I believe this assignment can only be carried out by you."

Jacob frowned in confusion.

"The princess," Prince Christopher began and this time, Jacob was sure he hadn't managed to keep his face expressionless given the small smile that played around the prince's face. "It's as I thought then," he muttered more to himself than to Jacob.

"The princess has decided that she'd like to travel to England. Lydia, that is to say the Countess Huntsforth, is expecting."

It certainly wasn't common for gentlemen to discuss such things, yet Jacob was too intrigued to worry about propriety, and clearly the prince had no scruples about it.

"Princess Harriet wants to be there to see the babe. And you and I both know that forbidding it will only put her in danger."

Wasn't that the truth? Jacob shuddered to think of what she'd manage to get herself into trying to sneak to another country.

He'd rather lock her in that tower he'd threatened her with the night of her sort of rescue.

"Indeed," he managed, for the prince seemed to be awaiting an answer.

"I need someone to escort her. To keep her safe. To take care of her. And that someone has to be you."

Jacob's heart soared before it plummeted.

Spending all that time alone with Harriet was like a gift from the gods.

But it didn't change the fact that the second son of a count wouldn't ever be able to have her.

"Forgive me, Your Highness. But why does it have to be me?" he asked, torn between taking the prince up on his offer before he changed his mind, though it was more order than offer, and running as far and as fast as he could.

"I cannot allow Harriet to flit off to other countries alone," the prince said frankly. "Yet, I know her stubbornness well enough to know that I cannot really stop her."

Jacob couldn't stifle his quick grin.

The prince knew his sister.

"The Crown Princess cannot be on a boat for weeks on end either alone or with a man, even if he is there as her guard. I spoke to my father. We are in complete agreement."

Now Jacob was confused again. Did the prince *not* want him escorting Harriet?

"Lauer, I'm going to ask you a question. I want an honest answer. Not because I am soon to be your king, but because I am Harriet's older brother and I care very deeply about what happens to her."

Jacob felt that damned cravat-noose tighten once more.

But he held the prince's gaze, refusing to drop his own.

"Do you love her?"

The question brought his heart to a dead stop.

He waited eons before answering, trying to weigh up what to say and how to say it.

In the end, he knew only honesty would do.

"I do," he said simply, but with feeling. "Desperately."

He expected the prince to throw him in the dungeon. Maybe challenge him to a duel. At least land him a facer.

To Jacob's surprise, however, the other man merely smiled.

"And that is why you are the only one who can carry out this assignment," he said. "Because what I said is true. Harriet cannot go to England with just a guard. But she can go with a husband."

Chapter Twenty-Four

*H*ARRIET SANK TO the floor with a sigh.

It was ridiculous that she'd stayed here this long hoping to catch a glimpse of Jacob when he left again.

This was precisely why she needed to get out of Aldonia for a time.

She needed to put an ocean between herself and the memories of Jacob.

Oh, but she'd miss him.

The sound of approaching footsteps interrupted her maudlin thoughts, and she looked up to see Jacob striding toward her.

With a gasp, she sprang to her feet, hastily straightening her pale pink skirts.

He kept coming until he was only inches from her, his jaw clenched, his eyes blazing with the brightest blue flame.

"Jacob." Her voice was breathless, but there wasn't

a thing she could do about it. "A-are you well?" she asked when he didn't speak.

"I've just been in a meeting with your brother," he said by way of answer. "He tells me you desire to travel to England."

Harriet rolled her eyes.

"Did he also tell you that I'm going to go whether he 'allows' it or not?" she bit out.

Truly, if he was here to lecture her just as Christopher and her father had done, then he could turn around and march right back out.

"He did, as it happens," Jacob answered.

"Oh." She blinked. "Well, good."

"You know, I have been in some of the most dangerous situations you could possibly imagine throughout my career working for your brother," he said conversationally.

She was surprised at the change in direction of the conversation, so she just stared at him.

"I've been stabbed, shot, beaten to a bloody pulp."

Harriet gasped at the horror of what he was saying.

"None of them have given me as much heartache as having to take care of you."

Well! That was just downright insulting.

She narrowed her eyes at him, then clenched her teeth as his grin made an appearance.

"And now, I'm told I'll have to do it all over again."

She'd been working up to delivering a set down of epic proportions, so it took a moment for his words to sink in.

"Wait. You – what?" she asked.

"The prince has just informed me that my next assignment is to escort you to England. Deliver you safely to your brother."

"Deliver me safely?" she asked hotly. "As though I am some package to be sent on the mail boat? How dare you? How dare *he?*"

Jacob leaned back against the glass, folding his arms and crossing his feet as though settling in to listen to her rant.

"When are you—all of you—going to get it through your stupid, overbearing heads that I am a woman grown? That I am perfectly capable of making my own plans and my own journeys. I don't need Christopher telling me what to do. And I don't need an overprotective, irritating, immature guard, for that matter."

To her horror, she felt tears spring into her eyes.

She'd been so happy to see him, yet nothing had changed.

He'd told her he loved her, but still he was treating her as nothing more than an assignment.

It was too badly done.

"I agree."

His words took her by surprise and stopped her ever-worsening thoughts on the spot.

"You – agree?" she repeated.

"I agree," he said again. "And what's more, your brother agrees."

Harriet could only stare at him while her brain tried to catch up.

"So then—you're *not* to come?"

It was foolish in the extreme to be saddened by this. Especially because only moments ago she'd been ranting and raving about having him as her guard.

But the disappointment was acute.

"Sweetheart." He stepped closer, causing her heart to flutter alarmingly. "Your brother knows you well enough to know you'll go to England whether he allows it or not."

Harriet could barely breathe with him standing so close.

She could smell the sandalwood scent that drove her wild, could see the flecks of silver in his eyes.

"And I know you well enough to know you'll put yourself in mortal danger trying to leave."

His scowl of disapproval was enough to make her almost feel sheepish. Almost.

"But of course, you cannot travel for weeks on end with a male guard for company. What would people think?"

She didn't give a hoot what people thought, though of course, she knew she should.

"No, after careful consideration your brother and I—and even your father—are in agreement."

"You are?" she asked carefully.

"We are." He nodded. "The only way this will possibly work will be if I come with you, not as your guard—"

He paused, and Harriet felt her stomach clench in anticipation.

"But as your husband."

His words turned her knees to liquid. It was a very good thing that he chose that moment to wrap her in his arms, for she wasn't sure she'd have stayed upright otherwise.

"M-my husband?" she stuttered.

"Indeed. Prince Christopher thought it was for the best, given the circumstances."

"And you?" she asked, hardly believing this was real.

"Me? Oh, I thought it was for the best, since I love you so much the mere thought of not being with you is excruciating. I'd walk through the fires of Hell to be your husband, sweetheart. Crossing an ocean will be child's play."

A burst of elation so intense, so pure, exploded within Harriet that she could do nothing but throw her arms around him and hold on as he lifted her from the floor and held her impossibly close.

"Does this mean you agree to your brother's terms?" he asked, his voice muffled against her hair.

Harriet pulled back so they were eye-to-eye.

"I do." She grinned. "If only because it saves me having a guard."

She laughed at his growl.

"And because I love you, too, Jacob. With all my

heart."

At her words, his eyes lit with as intense a love as she'd seen before he bent his head and took her mouth in an explosive kiss.

Indeed, anyone who saw them from the courtyard below was sure to be scandalised. Yet Harriet could not bring herself to care.

When she became lightheaded, he let her up for air, placing her on her feet yet keeping her deliciously close.

"You know, this is to be my last foreign mission. Or mission of any kind, really," he said, smiling down at her.

"It is?" She couldn't keep the smile of delight from her face. "But what will you do?"

"You are looking at the new head of Prince Christopher's special service agents," he said. "Based right here in the palace. Or wherever else you want to be."

"I want to be wherever you are," she answered promptly, earning herself another swift yet fierce kiss.

"So, this is your last assignment?" she asked. "Taking me to England."

"My last assignment," he confirmed. "Protecting the princess. And the only assignment I'll ever care about from here on? Being your husband and spending every day showing you just how much I love my wife."

"Now that assignment, I'll allow." She grinned before reaching up to press her lips once more against his own.

Epilogue

$\mathcal{T}$HE BALLROOM SPARKLED with thousands of candles as the state of Aldonia celebrated the wedding of their beloved princess.

Though there had been speculation amongst the subjects that the next royal to marry after Prince Alexander would be Prince Christopher, there was nothing but joy when Princess Harriet's betrothal was announced.

And only months later, the wedding occurred.

For the first time since Prince Alexander's wedding celebration, the entire royal family were in attendance, including Prince Alexander and Princess Lydia, who had arrived with their firstborn, the newest member of Aldonian royalty, Prince Frederick.

Outside the palace, the streets were alive with dancing and music and laughter.

Inside the palace walls, the mood was a little more sedate, but no less happy.

Harriet couldn't keep the smile from her face as she danced in the arms of her husband.

Though the ballroom was packed with royalty and dignitaries from all over Europe, she felt as though they were the only two people in the world.

"What are you thinking?" she asked her husband. Husband! How wonderful that sounded.

He stared down at her, looking so besotted that she felt herself blush.

"I'm just wondering how I got to be so lucky," he answered, his eyes smoldering.

"And well you might," she answered tartly. "You were really the most impossible man. I don't know how I put up with you."

"Me?" he exclaimed. "You were the impossible one! Walking yourself into trees when you weren't swinging out of them. I don't know how I kept from strangling you."

Harriet scowled at him but couldn't quite keep her serious expression. She was far too happy.

"Perhaps you are regretting your decision?" she suggested.

Jacob pulled her scandalously close and chuckled softly at her gasp.

"The only thing I regret," he whispered in her ear, setting off a raging storm of longing inside her. "Is not dragging you off somewhere to elope. Just you and I. And a bed."

Harriet could feel her cheeks burn but she couldn't deny that right at that moment, nothing sounded better.

"There isn't long left," she said, a little breathlessly. "And then we can leave."

"And you'll tell me where you've decided you want to go?" he asked, pressing a scandalous kiss to her neck before straightening and acting every inch the gentleman. But Harriet could still see the devilment in the depths of his eyes.

"Now that Lydia and Alex are here with little Freddie, England seems a bit pointless."

"I don't want to go to England," she said mischievously.

"And you won't want to be gone from the baby for too long," he said, watching her face for clues.

"No, I won't want to be gone too long. Just a couple of weeks will suffice."

The dance came to a close, but they didn't notice. They were too entwined in each other to notice anything else.

"So, what did you have in mind then?" he finally asked. "And how long will it take to get there?" he tagged on, a little desperately.

"An old, run down little cottage in the woods." She smiled, shivering at the delight and desire in his eyes.

"That's a two-day journey," he said huskily.

"Yes, but this time we can take a luxurious carriage" she promised. "With no other passengers except us two."

Jacob had a lot to learn about being a royal, Harriet supposed. One of which being that it was quite frowned upon to leave one's own wedding, dragging one's wife along as though the hounds of Hell were closing in fast.

But when they finally reached the privacy of their rooms, and he locked the door with a decisive click, she found that she preferred his way of doing things after all.

The End.

Dear Reader,

Thank you for reading *Protecting the Princess*! I hope you enjoyed Jacob and Harriet's journey to happily ever after. If you enjoyed this story please leave a quick review on your favorite book retailer. Reviews help other readers determine to try my books or not, and I love reading what you thought! If you want to learn about my new releases, or when my books go on sale, please follow me on BookBub, or subscribe to my newsletter.

Keep reading for a special preview of *Redeeming a Royal,* coming May/June 2020!

Redeeming A Royal

Nadine Millard

Heavy is the heart that wears the crown…

Prologue

"CHRISTOPHER, ARE YOU listening?"

Christopher Emmanuelle Farago Wesselbach dragged his gaze from the window and back to his father who was looming over him looking less than please.

The king never liked it when people got distracted in his presence. Least of all his own son.

And especially when it was his eldest son and therefore heir to the throne of Aldonia.

Christopher's father wasn't unkind or cruel. He was just king first, father second. That was how it needed to be. That was how Christopher himself would need to be when he ascended to the throne to rule their country.

As a boy of twelve, he knew this. Had known since he'd old enough to begin his lessons.

Crown and country first. Everything else second. Just as it should be.

Outside his father's personal study, a study that would one day belong to Christopher, his siblings Alexander and Harriet played noisily, their screeches and laughter floating on the summer breeze.

Christopher felt a pang of envy as he listened to them.

They sounded like they were having great fun. While he was stuck in here. Again.

When he'd been younger, his mother had tried to convince the king that Christopher should be given time to just be a boy, just be a child. But the king wouldn't hear of it.

"I had to learn. My father had to learn before me. And now, Christopher will learn. Duty to the crown must begin now."

And so, every day when the nannies and governesses and tutors took Alex and Hari on nature walks, and fishing expeditions, when they played in the garden, or swam in the lake, Christopher stayed inside the palace. Learning his duty. Preparing for his future.

"Later today we will meet with the captain of the guard," his father droned on, unaware of the direction that Christopher's self-pitying thoughts. "It won't be long before you will join the regiment. And the crown prince will be expected to know his role well."

"Yes, father," Christopher dutifully answered.

A sudden knock on the door sounded and his father's personal assistant hurried in with a silver tray carrying a single letter.

"A missive from the Duke of Tallenburg, sire," the man said with a bow.

Relations with the Tallenburg side of the family were strained. Even hostile. And Christopher, while not privy to the conversations just yet, was aware of it. One of the things he'd need to learn, his father had warned him, was how to deal with hostility in a calm and astute manner.

A good king ruled through respect, not fear, his father had said.

A great king honoured the privilege of his position while all the while remembering that he was there as a servant to the people. He worked for them, not the other way around.

Yes, his father was a wise and wonderful king. And Christopher always worried that he'd fall short when his turn came.

The king opened the letter, his eyes scanning the missive.

His face gave nothing away. No matter the task, no matter the challenge, his father's stoicism could always be relied upon.

It made him slightly cold, but always dependable.

"This will need to be addressed with some urgency," his father spoke to the assistant who hovered with the tray. "Arrange a meeting and make preparations for a short trip."

The servant bowed deferentially before swiftly exiting the office.

"I'm afraid that we shall have to reschedule our

meeting with the captain, Christopher."

"Of course, father," he answered at once.

The king studied him before his face suddenly softened into a rare smile.

"Why don't you spend the afternoon with your brother and sister?"

Christopher wanted to grin. Wanted to leap to his feet and rush from the room.

But he knew better.

He stood slowly, issuing a perfectly respectable bow to his father. The king.

"Thank you, father," he said sombrely before walking at a sedate pace out of the office and into the corridor outside.

It was only when he reached the staircase that Christopher allowed himself to smile.

He dashed down the stairs and ran full pelt for the gardens.

Perhaps he'd join whatever game Alex was playing with Hari.

Christopher didn't have the bond with his siblings that they had with each other. He'd been kept too distant from them. He'd been too busy learning to be a king to ever really get the chance to be a brother and a play mate. And much as he tried not to feel envious of their relationship, sometimes he wished that he was included in it, too.

Now, with his unexpected freedom, he would play

the rambunctious sword games that Alex favoured. And he would chase Harriet until she squealed and laughed like she did with Alex.

Christopher reached the garden, a grin on his face.

But as he watched, Alex and Harriet were led back to the palace by their nannies.

His smile faded as the garden emptied and Christopher stood in the middle of it. All alone.

He felt his eyes fill with childish tears and refused to let them fall.

He was the crown prince. Heir to the throne. One day, he would be king.

He didn't need play time in the garden. He didn't need the company of his brother, or sister, or anyone else.

He just needed to stay focused so that one day, he'd be a good and just ruler.

Crown and country came first. Everything else came second.

If you enjoyed this, look for *Redeeming a Royal,* set to release May/June 2020! To learn about my new releases, please follow me on BookBub, or subscribe to my newsletter.

Acknowledgements

Thank you to my wonderful readers first and foremost for continuing on this journey with me! It's a wild ride and I never want it to stop.

Thanks to my husband and children who are the reason I do everything. Your support and pride in me is what keeps me going.

To my parents, my sisters, and all my friends and family who never fail to support me and keep my spirits up! And the authors who always have my back.

Finally a huge thank you to my editor, Julie—the best partner a girl could have, and everyone at Aurora Publicity for making something great from my chaos!

Also by Nadine Millard
International Best-Seller

The Ranford Series
An Unlikely Duchess
Seeking Scandal
Mysterious Miss Channing

The Revenge Series
Highway Revenge
The Spy's Revenge
The Captain's Revenge

The Saints & Sinners Series
The Monster of Montvale Hall
The Angel of Avondale Abbey
The Devil of Dashford Manor
The Saint of St. Giles

Standalone Romances
A Winter Wish (Forbidden – A Regency Collection)
A Christmas Seduction
Christmas At Brentwood Abbey
Beauty and the Duke
The Hidden Prince
His Yuletide Bride
Fortune Favors Miss Gold

Coming Soon!

Redeeming a Royal
The Cowboy's Wager
Lady Holly's Jolly Christmas
Her Accidental Groom
A Country Christmas

A Lord For All Seasons
Springtime Scandal
Midsummer Madness
Forgotten Fall
A Winter Wedding

About Nadine Millard

Nadine Millard is a bestselling writer hailing from Dublin, Ireland.

When she's not writing historical romance, she's managing her chaotic household of three children, a husband and a very spoiled dog!

She's a big fan of coffee and wine with a good book and will often be found at her laptop at 2am when a book idea strikes.

Connect with Nadine!
Website: nadinemillard.com
Newsletter: subscribepage.com/nadinemillard
BookBub: bookbub.com/authors/nadine-millard
Amazon: amazon.com/Nadine-Millard/e/B00JA9OXFK
Facebook: facebook.com/nadinemillardauthor
Instagram: instagram.com/nadinemillardauthor

Made in the USA
Middletown, DE
19 September 2021